DAWN OF DARKNESS

DAWN OF DARKNESS

A NEW DAWN™ BOOK TWO

AMY HOPKINS

MICHAEL ANDERLE

LMBPN

DISRUPTIVE IMAGINATION®

From Amy

*To my husband, whose expression every time I talk about writing
inspired every look of male confusion in this book.
With thanks to all the coffee producers in the world. Without you, this
book would not have happened.*

From Michael

*To Family, Friends and
Those Who Love To Read.
May We All Enjoy Grace
To Live The Life We AreCalled.*

CHAPTER ONE

Cold air tickled Julianne's arm, causing her to shiver. *It's cold tonight,* she thought sleepily as she pulled the blanket up under her chin. Outside, an owl's call floated across the dark sky just before a scream shattered the still night.

Julianne bolted out of bed, stumbling into the room next door. On one of the cots, a man sat, his eyes flickering back and forth as he sucked in deep, desperate breaths. He screamed again, and Julianne grabbed his shoulders.

"Harlon. *Harlon!*" she called out.

Her words caught his attention, but didn't break through. He turned, then lurched forward, toppling her over and pinning Julianne to the floor. He screamed again.

"*HARLON!*" Julianne yanked herself free and slapped the man across the face, desperate to wake him.

His scream was abruptly cut off, and he sank to the floor, his breathing quickly evening out to a steady pace. His large frame looked pitiful on the floor, dark hair matted down and face covered in sweat—nothing like the vibrant man Julianne had eaten dinner with earlier that evening.

The slap had jerked him from his nightmare, but hadn't

woken him. He was probably so exhausted from the string of bad dreams that it would take more than a quick sting to bring him to wakefulness.

"Come on, you big lug." Julianne squatted down and lifted Harlon's upper body, hoisting him up to her shoulders. Then, she staggered over to his bed. She leaned forward to let him down, but his weight toppled her over, and she landed on the mattress, the still unconscious man a dead weight on top.

"Dammit, Jules. I turn my back for five minutes and you're in bed with another man." Marcus stood at the door, peering in through the darkness.

"Fuck you." Julianne was ready to tear someone's eyes out after weeks of interrupted sleep and episodes like this one. "He's all yours tomorrow night. I don't care if I have to go spend the night in a cave."

"And I hope you had a lovely sleep, too, beautiful. He didn't hurt you, did he?" Marcus shoved Harlon to one side then took Julianne's hand and hoisted her up.

She shook her head. "No, he just scared the shit out of me and made sure that, yet again, I'm going to start another day in a foul mood. Bitch's honor, I'd kill for a full night's sleep."

"If he wakes again, I'll take him." Marcus wrapped an arm around her shoulder and pulled her close, pressing his lips to her forehead. "I'll make up an extra bed in the barn. It's warm enough out there that you'll be comfortable, and if you can put up with Garrett's snoring, you'll get a better night's sleep."

Julianne nodded, accepting his logic. Sleeping out with the rearick, the hired guards from their homeland, would at least stop her heart from jumping every time Harlon rolled over. "Thanks." She gave Marcus a gentle shove and sent him back to bed.

Julianne scowled at Harlon. She knew it wasn't his fault—it was a side-effect of the mind control he'd been under. When released from the spell, he and a small percentage of the other affected villagers had suffered side effects, things like raging migraines and night terrors.

Harlon was Annie's son, and Julianne felt she owed it to the old woman to help as much as she could. After defeating the New Dawn, Annie had insisted on putting them up, giving them a place to stay.

This was the sixth night in a row that Harlon had woken screaming. It didn't seem to be getting any better. Again and again, Julianne and everyone else in the small, crowded cottage was pulled from their slumber during the night by the man's screams. Her heart burned with sympathy, but even a mystic as powerful as Julianne had her limits.

Julianne glanced out the tiny window. The moon was almost full and hung low in the sky, painting white ripples on the barren field outside. It would need to be planted soon, before they missed the season. She chewed her lip as the thought of what lay ahead weighed on her mind.

Julianne rolled her shoulders and made to leave, but paused. She looked back, then tucked a corner of Harlon's blanket under his chin. After all, it was cold tonight.

CHAPTER TWO

Annie pursed her lips as she laid the table for breakfast. Hands on hips, she stepped back to admire the pristine gingham tablecloth, the neatly placed condiments and the pretty flowers poking out of a little vase in the middle.

"Best enjoy it while it's clean," she mumbled. "Because it won't be like it for long."

Harlon shuffled in, his dirty blonde hair matted on one side. "Morning, Ma."

"Pick your feet up, son, and stop dragging your ass about like it weighs too much. I know you're tired, but that's no excuse to walk like a worm-riddled dog." She softened her words with a smile and tipped her head towards the kitchen. "Bring out the hot food, will you?"

She stood by the table, mistress of her domain, and braced for the influx of people.

"Aye, what a bonnie sight ye are this mornin', Annie!" Garrett gave her a cheeky grin as he stomped straight past her, into the kitchen where he loaded his arms full of plates.

"Don't you drop those, rearick," Annie admonished. The stocky rearick was the shortest man she had ever seen, but he was strong as an ox. *An ox in a china shop,* she thought to herself wryly.

"Don't worry yerself, Annie." Bette, as squarely built and heavy footed as Garrett, went to help him. Between them, the two rearick managed to bring out all the food, Harlon trailing behind with a pitcher of milk. "Ye know I'd break his balls if he broke anything."

"You'd have to find them first!"

Annie whirled, startled by the new voice. Marcus winced. "Sorry. Didn't mean to make you jump, Annie." Now this man, he was no rearick. Tall and good looking, Annie could see why Julianne had set her eye on him. Why, if Annie were a little younger herself…

Francis poked his head out from behind Marcus. Annie hadn't noticed him follow the strapping young guard in. "Ma? You ok there?"

Annie blushed, but before she could answer, Marcus slid past with a wink. "I'd say your ma is mighty fine."

Annie raised an eyebrow. "I don't believe you mean that for a moment, you rapscallion." She eyed him as he sidled towards a seat and, as he got a bit closer, flicked his ass with her tea towel. She hid a smile when he yelped. "Wash first. You know the rules."

The rearick had been up since well before dawn, tending the cattle and horses. She had heard them clean up earlier, but both obliged her by lifting their spotless hands for inspection. She nodded. Her house might be full, but she still ran it, damned if she didn't.

"Good morning, Annie." As Julianne stepped out, a giant yawn cracked her jaw. She shrugged an apology as she slid into one of the chairs at the table.

"Morning, Julianne." Annie gave her a nod. "I've some fresh honey for the bread. I know how you like it."

Julianne's face softened into a smile. "You shouldn't have… but I'm glad you did. Thanks, Annie."

Danil and Bastian came down last, the two mystics already in their white robes. Danil's eyes, white as snow, no longer gave Annie the creeps. He, along with his companions, had more than proved themselves different from the mystics who had ravaged their little town.

Once they were all at the table, Annie glanced at each face at her table. The two rearick, Bette swatting Garrett's hand as he reached for a second sausage. Marcus, who was carefully lifting some sauerkraut onto Julianne's plate as she gave him a tired smile. Bastian, his head close to Danil's as they discussed their plans for the day as they went about trying to repair the village. Finally, her sons. Francis and Harlon sat quietly, eyes on the table.

"Here, Francis. Throw me one of them bread rolls, will ye?" Garrett called.

"Don't ye dare, lad," Bette interjected. "Ye'll make a right mess doin' that, and I know what yer mother will do to the lot of us if yer do."

The corner of Francis's mouth turned up, and he gave Annie a sideways glance. She pretended not to see.

Eyes twinkling, Francis lobbed the bread roll. If it had been anyone else, Annie would have called it bad luck brought on by bad manners. Francis, though, was a crack shot. If that bread roll landed straight in Garrett's milk, it was because he meant it to.

Garrett squealed like a neutered pig and jumped up, patting his beard and shaking the warm drink all over the table.

"Watch it, yer bloody oaf," Bette yelled. "I dinna want to wear yer damned drink!"

"It's not my fault!" Garrett said with a wounded look. "He's the wanker what threw it!"

Francis was silent, face in hands and shoulder shaking uncontrollably. Annie placed her hands on the table ready to leap to her feet, thinking it was some kind of seizure, until he gasped in a breath and erupted into laughter.

Garrett pegged a mushroom at Francis, hitting Harlon in the cheek by mistake. The big man barely reacted, digging his spoon into his porridge for another bite. A moment later, that 'bite' was stuck to Marcus's shirt.

"Oh, you're on," Marcus said.

Julianne scooted her chair back in alarm. "Don't!" she yelped. "That'll go ev—"

Too late. Marcus flicked his cup of milk at Harlon and the warm liquid showered everyone.

"Bitch help me," Danil moaned. "I know you're in love, Marcus, but spraying your milk all over the table is a bit much!"

"*Danil!*" Julianne snapped, her face bright red.

Annie chortled. That girl was cool as a cucumber in the face of battle. She didn't think she had ever seen Julianne rattled like *that*.

Danil ducked the first chunk of bread lobbed at his head, but then Julianne's eyes misted over to match his.

"What? No fair, blocking me is against—" his words were swallowed as Julianne darted up from the table and dumped a whole bowl of porridge on Danil's head.

By now, bits of food were flying across the table at lightning speed, and the tablecloth was more 'shades of sausage and gravy' than the red gingham it had been moments before.

Annie sat back, suspiciously free of the debris that whizzed past. When a bit of gravy splashed in front of her, everyone froze. Annie eyed them.

"As long as you all clean up after yourselves, I didn't see a damn thing." Picking up her plate, she stood and calmly walked out of the dining room.

As she placed it in the sink and ran the water over it, she wondered if, despite the trials facing them all, her house had ever been so full of happiness.

CHAPTER THREE

"No, stop trying so hard. It'll come to you, you just have to let it. Tessa, you look exhausted. Why don't you take a break?" Danil kept his voice even, relying on his many years of meditation to keep from losing his cool.

The three women in his class bowed politely, then left the room quickly. This was only their fourth lesson, but Danil was starting to feel the pressure. This wasn't the mystic Temple, where students had all the time they needed to hone their skills.

It was no more than a tiny, abandoned cottage, repurposed as a small magic school where the village inhabitants came for weekly lessons on how to shield, and where those with a talent for mental magic could learn to hone their skills.

If the New Dawn returned, the simple shields now known by most of the residents wouldn't be enough to stop them being brainwashed and enslaved again, so Danil pushed them hard.

The teachings of Ezekiel, the Founder who had taught the very first magic in the land, said that everyone possessed a spark of magic. Not everyone could harness it, though, and even those who could had no guarantee of being any good at it.

This meant that much of his efforts would be wasted trying to teach those with no skill, or who would never progress enough to shield with any degree of usefulness. Still, every person he could help was one that might be saved if the New Dawn launched another attack.

That is, if they could convince the villagers that what they were doing was important. So far, none had refused to come, but the effort they were putting in was more to humor the mystics than because they saw the importance of it.

"You're frustrated," Bastian commented.

"Well, that's stating the obvious," Danil snorted in return. "They're trying, I know that, but they're trying too damned hard."

"You don't think that has anything to do with the fact that they're shitting their pants waiting for another attack, and exhausted from trying to run the farms and look after their loved ones?" Bastian kept his face bland, turning so he didn't have to look Danil quite in the eye while he asked.

Danil might be blind, but it didn't make him any less intimidating when he was mad as a cut snake. It didn't help that he was Bastian's superior.

"What did you say, Bastian?" Danil asked.

Confused, Bastian shook his head. "I didn't say anything."

"How kind of you to offer!" Danil exclaimed, a grin spreading over his face.

"Offer? I didn't—"

"Oh? I could have *sworn* you just offered to take the next class, show off that sage wisdom a bit. Bloody good idea, my friend. I'll be down at the watering hole if you need me, eh?" Danil clapped Bastian on the shoulder and walked off, ignoring Bastian's curses. "Don't let anything interesting happen while I'm gone!" he shouted over his shoulder.

"Sly bastard," Bastian grumbled to himself when Danil was gone. "I can't believe I fell for that." He set about tidying the room, trying to ignore the butterflies in his stomach. He hadn't taught a class before—hell, he was only a student himself a few short months ago.

"Hello? Master Danil?" Bastian looked up to see Lilly at the door.

The little nature magician was barely nine, but three months spent hiding in the city streets as she watched her town fall apart had aged her beyond her years.

"Sorry, Lilly, you just missed him. I think he's gone off to find some lunch." Bastian pulled two more chairs into the circle, hoping that the five men Danil had pissed off last week would all return.

"Oh. I came to see if he still needed any help with the class. Is it not on, Master Bastian?"

Bastian frowned. "Lilly, please. Julianne is our only Master, and she's told you that you don't even have to call her that. We're not your masters, none of us are."

She ducked her head and turned to go.

"Wait! I mean... I'm taking the class." Bastian wiped sweaty palms on his robe, cursing his bad luck that it was this class Danil had stranded him with. "I'm taking the class today. You can go play for a bit if you like."

"Of course, Ma— err, Bastian."

He gave her a grateful smile as footsteps alerted him to the student's arrival.

"Master Bastian, Tollin is birthing one of his sheep, so he said to tell you he can't make it today." Francis twisted his hat in his hands as if expecting to be yelled at.

Bastian couldn't blame him. Last time, Danil had become so frustrated during their lesson he had nearly snapped the man's head off. He had a suspicion the sheep was more excuse than anything, but didn't push the issue.

"It's fine, Francis. You're all here by choice, you don't owe us an explanation if you miss a lesson." Bastian gestured to the seats. "And please, don't call me Master."

The men filed in and sat, looking around nervously. "Where's Danil?" Jarv asked gruffly.

"Couldn't make it," Bastian said without explaining.

"Got sick of us, did he? I don't blame him. We can't shield for shit." Mack leaned back in his chair, unworried. "If I were him, I wouldn't waste the time either."

"Then why are *you* here?" Bastian asked mildly.

"S'pose even a slim chance is better than none. If those bastards come back, I don't want to be licking their boots again. Rather kill myself first."

Bastian nodded. "Danil isn't sick of you; he's sick of himself. Back at the Temple, we go through these exercises over years, slowly coaxing the power out of people. It took me a whole season just to learn how to shut my bloody head up long enough for a basic meditation, and I was dying to learn."

"But you're an expert now, aren't you?" Mack asked. "I mean, you helped fight off those bastard Dawners."

"Barely," Bastian laughed. "I passed the last of my tests just before winter. I'm just a baby compared to Danil, and a worm next to Julianne." He left the honorific off her name, knowing she wanted the town folk to call her by name, not her title.

"So, he left the baby to teach us?" Jarv looked skeptical.

Bastian nodded, trying to act confident. "He's low on sleep, and mad as a bear. He knows his teaching skills are out of date because he hasn't held a class in over two years. And he knows that his failure is putting you at risk." Bastian met each man's eyes, one by one. "He's trying. Trying and failing. That's why he's so frustrated."

"He's a good man; we know that." Lewis spoke quietly. "Our heads might be broken, but we can see his heart is in the right place. Maybe that's why some of us snap back at him. We see him trying, and we just can't keep up."

Bastian pressed his lips together, breathing deeply. This was the most conversation either of the mystics had gotten out of any of the men, except maybe Francis. "Maybe we all need to take a step back. This isn't the kind of thing you can force."

Then, he narrowed his gaze on Lewis. "But you're not broken. Danil has examined all of you, cleared you for learning. We wouldn't be here otherwise. You four were the first to get that ok. You know what that means?"

The four men exchanged confused glances.

"You're strong. You had an entire group of psycho mind fuckers get in your heads, rummage around and screw things up in there. They did it for months! And despite that, you're still ok. Guys, that's incredible!" Bastian's voice rose as he let his excitement show.

Lewis frowned. "You sure you're not just saying that to make us feel less shitty about all this?"

Bastian raised his eyebrows and spread his hands, as if inviting Lewis to examine the proof himself.

"Boy has a point," Mack said. "Either way, I got a field what needs some work. We gonna do this or what?" He leaned forwards in his seat, face creasing as he tried to slip into a meditation.

Bastian bit his tongue, then cursed at himself. If Danil wants me to run this class, I'll damn well run it my way.

"Not like that," he said. Mack sat up, startled. "You're trying too hard. It's… it's like a pretty girl. You go in with a glower and start demanding she dance with you, you're gonna go home alone. You have to ease in, gently."

"Last time Mack eased into a girl she threw him off a building," Jarv snorted. "What, you never wondered why he was so ugly? She rearranged his face!"

Mack did have an unusually asymmetrical face. Bastian let out a chuckle, but stopped at Mack's sad look of defeat. "Wait. You mean he wasn't joking?"

"Oh, it weren't like that! Her pa came home early, and she was so eager to hide me, she weren't still in the downstairs bedroom."

He grimaced as Bastian laughed even harder. "Broke my nose and half my jaw on some stupid statue her Ma had on the front lawn."

Bastian's lungs heaved, trying to catch his breath. "Bitch's britches, Mack. That's the funniest thing I've ever heard!"

Mack turned up one corner of his mouth, a smile that had just a hint of pride to it. "I dare say so, Bastian. I dare say so."

"Old papa Jefferson felt so bad he paid the surgeon to fix it up and didn't even cut his balls off for diddling his daughter," Francis piped up. "Now, *that's* an achievement to be proud of. When Jefferson caught young Hannity in her room, the kid came out with one bean halfway to his throat and the other one in his left boot, and I don't think he ate sausages for a year after."

With that, the whole room fell into loud, raucous laughter. "Oh, hell, I'm glad Lilly wasn't here for that one," Bastian whimpered as he wiped the tears from his face.

By the time they had themselves under control, their lesson time was half over.

"So, we just ease into it, right?" Lewis asked.

Bastian nodded.

"Sounds easy. Or it would if I knew what the fuck that meant," Jarv grumbled.

Bastian sighed. Danil had been driving most of the students, but these men especially. As victims of the mind control spell the New Dawn had mastered, they were the most vulnerable if it happened again. After a forced period of rest, they had been deemed strong enough to try using the magic that was innate to all.

However, their eagerness and Danil's impatience both worked against the magic itself. Mental magic required a calm mind, an inner stillness that was more elusive the harder it was fought for.

"Let's try something different," Bastian said. He thought back to the very first time he used mental magic.

It had been after class. A month of training, trying as hard as these men to force his will over something elusive and intangible.

Finally, one afternoon it had happened, and not at all how he had expected.

Tired, crabby and sick of the press of people that always seemed to be around, he had snuck off up the mountain. He hadn't gone far, just enough that the air didn't smell like bread and the view over the Temple made it look like another world.

He had made himself comfortable in the crook of a tree branch and almost fell asleep, listening to the birds and letting his mind drift. That's when it had happened—a sense of oneness had crept over him as his breathing settled and the universe became just an extension of his fingertips.

Bastian blinked, clearing his suddenly-white eyes and letting go of his magic.

"Let's try it with whiskey," Mack suggested.

Bastian grinned. "Actually…" He walked over to Annie's liquor cabinet and pulled out a bottle of amber liquid. "I'm not getting you drunk, just loosening things up a bit."

He poured a shot for each of them and watched each man down it with pleasure. Francis had told him a few days ago that the New Dawn had destroyed most of the alcohol in the village, probably because it could make the effects of mind control unpredictable.

"Now, instead of trying to make the magic happen, let's take a few minutes to meditate. You've been practicing every day, haven't you?" He eyed the men.

Mack looked away, pretending to examine the drapes. Lewis shrugged. Jarv grinned and nodded eagerly and Francis stayed quiet, knowing as well as Bastian did that he hadn't practiced once.

"That's fine," Bastian said easily.

Mack, Lewis, and Francis let out sighs of relief, glad to be spared the tongue lashing Danil was prone to giving when they admitted they hadn't been putting any extra effort into learning to shield.

They settled back in their chairs, eyes closed, hands limp in their laps. One minute passed, then another as Bastian skimmed their minds.

It was no surprise they had trouble letting go of their thoughts. Each man had been through so much pain and loss over the previous months. Bastian withdrew from Jarv's mind, which was surprisingly clear and right on the edge of expanding into a true meditation. He didn't want to inadvertently distract him at the critical moment.

He pushed his mind out to Francis, whose face was pulled into a slight frown as he tried to force his mind blank. Bastian watched him push thoughts of his wife away over and over again.

Danielle had been mind-controlled into thinking the growth in her throat was cured by the New Dawn. Bastian knew that wasn't possible, not for someone with mental magic. Healing was the realm of the druids.

She had died just a few days after Julianne and her people had liberated the town, the growth now so large it strangled her. Francis had laid her body, thin and frail after two weeks of being unable to swallow, to rest in the small family graveyard. He had vowed to destroy the New Dawn if it killed him to do it.

I will burn them for what they did, Francis thought, unaware that Bastian was listening in.

Uncomfortable eavesdropping, Bastian pulled away just as Francis's fingers twitched. As Bastian turned back to Mack, something sparked in the corner of his sight. He looked back to see a tiny flame flickering in Francis's upturned palm.

"Fuck!" Francis snatched his hand up and shook it, his eyes wide with panic. Bastian missed the telltale change in color that happened when someone used physical magic like that. "What the fuck was that?"

The others jumped and when Bastian, bemused at the turn of events, looked to Mack, his heart gave an excited thump. The man's eyes glowed white.

"Uh, Mack? You feeling ok there, bud? You look a bit…" Jarv's face was almost as white as Mack's eyes, which cleared as he focused on his friend.

"What?" Mack asked, seemingly unaware of what he'd just done.

It was too much for Bastian, who felt a bubble of laughter rise from his belly. His four students looked on as their teacher dissolved into hysterical laughter.

"Danil…" he gasped, wiping tears from his eyes. "Danil will *never* believe I got two of you to cast magic!"

CHAPTER FOUR

Artemis paced back and forth, the small, abandoned stable only giving him a few steps to move each way. His feet kicked at the bedroll jumbled in a heap on the straw and Julianne wondered, not for the first time, why he had chosen to sleep there.

If she thought he was capable of feeling guilt, she would have guessed that was the reason. Artemis, though, didn't feel things like normal people. He wasn't a bad man. Just… wired differently.

Julianne hadn't known him back at the Temple, but some of her friends had. They'd warned her he was different, that even though his heart was usually in the right place, he had trouble showing it.

His mind was a mess of information. Memories, facts, musings and questions leaked out of his brain as if there was so much to ponder, he couldn't keep it all in. His passion was for information. People were just things that either provided it, or didn't.

"Because I can't abide people," he snapped, reading her thoughts. When he looked up, his white eyes seemed surprised. *You don't think I like being back here, do you? Surrounded by people with their noisy lips and shouty heads, interrupting my peace!*

19

The mental sending struck Julianne sharply, the clear thought forming a hard edge in the man's otherwise scattered mind. For all the time she had spent trying to understand his mind and make sense of the way his thoughts fluttered around like a cloud of butterflies, she was no closer.

"Artemis, it has nothing to do with liking people. It's about what's right," Julianne said patiently.

"Right for who?" he quipped. "Certainly not right for me. No, what's right for me is disappearing, vanishing into the woods and never coming back. Just think, Julianne. If I'd done that to begin with, none of this would have happened!"

"We've been through this!" Julianne snapped. "It doesn't matter what you did. You never meant to kick off such wide-spread destruction, I understand that. But you bloody well need to do your part in fixing it."

It wasn't like she was asking much. She, Danil, and Bastian had their hands full trying to teach the townspeople how to create mental shields. Without that vital skill, they were defenseless against future attacks by the mystics who had enslaved them before.

She put her hand on her hips and drew herself up. "Artemis, your place with the mystic community *depends* on it."

Artemis stilled. He opened his mouth, then closed it. Finally, he slumped. "Fine. I'll help. On one condition."

Julianne raised an eyebrow. He wasn't exactly in a bargaining position. Still, she didn't want him offside, so she nodded for him to proceed.

"I'll take three classes a week, no more. Children only. They don't argue as much as their parents."

Julianne hesitated, then nodded. It was all she had intended to ask of him, but she would let him think it was a win.

Artemis stepped closer. "And one lesson for you, and one for your friends. You will let me test you. And, maybe, try some things I've been working on."

Julianne sighed. Artemis had been badgering her to let him test her strength for weeks now. She wanted to—she was just as curious as he seemed to be. She just hadn't had the time.

"You'll take four lessons with the children, and one per week with each of us. Fair?"

Artemis grinned and nodded eagerly. "Wonderful. The other two can double up, they're not particularly interesting. I can't wait to get in your head, though!"

Julianne shook her head in exasperation. Artemis had a knack with words that would send most people around the bend. "Whatever you say, Artemis. Just… try to be nice to the children at least?"

He shrugged, his innocent expression so earnest it was almost comical. "I adore children. It's their parents I can't stand."

CHAPTER FIVE

"Higher. *Higher*, ye soft-cocked little man!" Bette heaved her side of the barrel, trying to lift it into the cart.

"Hang on, the stench is so bad I canna breathe. Just..." Garrett's grip failed, and the large tub started to topple. He snatched at it with both hands, jerking it too high in his haste to catch it. "Look out!" he yelled.

His warning came far too late. The carefully harvested pile of cow, horse, and sheep droppings slipped to the ground, the wooden barrel exploding on impact. He flinched as dung splattered his face, then cowered as a shit-covered figure rose before him.

"I... will... *KILL*... YOU..." Bette growled. She used her shirt to scrub at her face, but it was as dirty as the rest of her. She spat, almost gagged, then stripped off her shirt. The linen chemise beneath it was only marginally cleaner. "And stop looking at me tits, ye clumsy bastard. I know yer doin' it."

She finally found a clean strip of cloth to wipe her eyes and glared at Garrett. Bette kicked at a pile of dung on the ground, splattering it over his pants, then stormed off.

Garrett watched her go, eyes wide. "Oh, I'm in the shit now," he muttered, then laughed at his own pun.

"What in the Bastard's name is that stink?" Danil laughed when Garrett jumped at his voice. "Sorry, friend. Didn't mean to startle you. What's wrong? You look like you're expecting the hangman's noose. And what's that smell?" He screwed up his face, sniffing the air.

"Get fucked," Garrett growled. "Ye've read it in me mind already, haven't ye? Ye just wanna rub it in by making me say it out loud."

Danil laughed. "You got me there. I caught Bette's thoughts on her way out, too. Bloody glad I'm not in your shoes."

"Aye, well, you be getting out of me head, ye cheeky prick." Garrett scraped his boot on the bottom of the wagon, only succeeding in spreading the mess around. "Ahh fuck. I'll have to shovel this shit back up meself. She's not coming back, is she?"

"I doubt it," Danil said with a laugh. "But can you blame her?"

He lifted one of the shovels from the cart and tentatively began to load it with dung. He used his magic to look through Garrett's eyes, but politely stayed away from the rearick's deeper thoughts.

It was slow work, as Danil had to pause each time the rearick looked away, but they soon fell into a rhythm.

"Thank ye, Danil. I do appreciate the help, even if yer an asshole."

"Anytime, you snarky little bastard," Danil replied dryly.

Garrett grinned at him. "While it's just us," he began, looking around to make sure that was true, "I thought maybe ye might have a wee bit of advice for me."

Danil raised an eyebrow, wondering what he was about to get himself into.

"Well," Garrett continued. "It's about... well, it's about womenfolk. Ye seem like ye may have a bit more experience with 'em than I do, if ye know what I mean."

Danil laughed. "I doubt that. I mean sure, I live with a bunch of them and I've dated my fair share, but that doesn't mean I understand them." Even his mind reading ability didn't eliminate that hurdle.

"Go on with ye," Garrett groaned. "I thought you at least would know."

"Life in the Temple… it's different to the outside. Less complicated, for the most part. Fewer misunderstandings due to this"—Danil tapped his head—"and we do tend to have more leniency towards casual flings than the outside world. Still, women? You're asking the wrong man, my friend."

"Bah. Well, I'll ask ye anyway, because Marcus is too bloody smitten with Julianne to be of any damned use." Garrett stood back and scratched his beard. "I've been fixin' to ask Bette a question, the sort that a man can't just come out and ask a lass."

A grin almost cracked Danil's face in half. "Oh, I know exactly the sort of question." He clapped Garrett over the shoulder. "And I know exactly what to do."

"Ye do?" Garrett asked warily. "Because I like me balls round and intact, if ye know what I mean."

"Oh, I know," Danil said.

He winced as he contemplated just what punishment an angry Bette would dish out to an unsuspecting rearick. Bette was a firecracker, and no one bore the brunt of that more than Garrett.

The two men scraped the last of the mess off the ground, conversation stalled as they carefully lifted it up on the cart. They managed to do it without a repeat of the earlier attempt and Danil stood back as Garrett strapped it in securely.

"Look," Danil said. "I've had an idea brewing in the back of my head for the last few days, and it might just be the answer to your problem… and to a few others, not to mention being a shit-ton of fun. If you help me out with it, I'll make sure you get the perfect opportunity to ask Bette that question of yours."

Garrett narrowed his eyes, knowing Danil had a love of mischief. Still, he figured it would all be worth it if Bette said yes.

CHAPTER SIX

Julianne left the stable as close to a run as she could without being obvious. Artemis meant well, but he could talk the ear off a drunk raccoon. She wondered if he would have even noticed if she had snuck out twenty minutes earlier. Admittedly, she probably wouldn't have cared if he did.

Even now, his voice rambled on to no one in particular as he contemplated the physiological difference that caused each type of magic to affect the eyes differently. So far, he hadn't managed to crack the code, and it bothered him greatly.

Mystics' eyes turned white when using their powers, while nature mages' eyes were green. Physical magic turned a caster's eyes an eerie black and recently, another type of magic had been discovered that made the girl's eyes glow a violent shade of red.

That had been startling to see, not least because Bethany Anne, believed to be the first magic user, had been depicted with red eyes. Though the records never did agree on where she went exactly, she had left earth hundreds of years ago, and her legend was one of the most prolific in this new age.

Bethany Anne's departure had eventually spawned the Age of Madness, a period where the elements that connected humans with magic sent them mad. Thanks to the Founder—who had ended the period of darkness and returned to teach people like Julianne's old Master, Selah, how to use magic again—the world was finally coming to rights.

Still, the power they had was far from what Bethany Anne, also known as the Queen Bitch, was known to do. Immortal, invincible and yet still full of compassion (at least according to the legends), she was most often depicted with glowing red eyes.

Julianne made a mental note to tell Artemis about Hannah, the young girl Ezekiel had found with unheard of powers and crimson eyes.

She spared a quick wave to Danil, who was deep in conversation with Garrett, then wrinkled her nose at the smell. They must be off to cart the animal castings to a neighboring farm for composting.

Annie had a magical talent for growing things, a tiny sliver of untrained nature magic that eliminated the need for fertilizing and extra water.

The town was still reeling after months of neglect. The New Dawn had pillaged the harvests and taken everything of value. Whether they had only planned to stay until they had run the place down, or were just incredibly stupid, she wasn't yet sure.

Maybe today's examination will finally shed some light on that, she thought.

Fifteen minutes later, she arrived at an old stone wheelhouse. She waved at Josh, the guard out front. "Is Marcus here?" she called.

He raised a hand to his head as he thumped his chest, a salute some of the townspeople had taken for the mystics. Though Josh's hair was as white as the cotton wool clouds overhead, he stood tall and proud. "Yes, ma'am. Inside with the muckers."

Julianne pressed her lips together at the insulting term. She knew the townspeople didn't think of Julianne and her friends as muckers—a term coined from the shortening of 'mind fuckers'—but she had been on the pointy end of hate for mystics before.

She chose to ignore it, though, figuring the people who used it had been treated badly enough by the 'muckers' to call them whatever they damn well wanted to.

The old wooden door creaked as she pushed it open. It was dark inside, the tiny windows at the top of the building filtering the only spears of light with dirty glass and muddy streaks.

"Oh, for goodness sake, Marcus. I know it's meant to be a containment center, but you don't need to make it look like a dungeon." Julianne squinted into the shadows to where Marcus lazily leaned against a wall.

"It's not me," Marcus said with a shrug. "They're still punishing themselves. If you want the lantern, it's over there." He gestured to the wall beside the door Julianne had come through.

Her shoulders dropped. "Not again," she mumbled.

The last remaining members of the New Dawn were like a thorn digging into her foot. Sure, they were scum, but not quite the level of scum that August, Rogan's second in command, had forced them to be.

"Present!" Marcus barked.

The full figures, almost hidden by the dark shadows in the room, stood swiftly and saluted. It wasn't the tap to the head and fist to the heart that Julianne's people were familiar with. Instead, they slowly raised a hand then stiffly touched one ear, a gesture she knew they'd been taught by August.

"If I may speak, Master?" A man stepped forwards, shoulders slouched and eyes to the ground.

Julianne bit back an impatient report. "Of course, Jeffery. You know you don't need to ask permission to speak."

"Thank you, wise leader."

Julianne rolled her eyes. The group she faced had a clear split of personalities: those that resisted any attempt to show respect towards her, and those who layered it on thicker than the shit that had filled Garrett's barrel earlier.

"Danil was by earlier. Said my head is as good as any. I'd like to request to be the next to submit to sentencing."

Julianne bristled. The prisoners called it sentencing, though anyone who referenced the procedure around her was careful to use the word 'examination'. She didn't bother arguing with Jeffrey. Not just because it wouldn't do any good, but because, in a way, he was right.

"Very well." Julianne ignored the slightly surprised and overly fearful look on Jeffery's face. "Marcus, bring him to the room, and we'll get started right away."

"My pleasure," Marcus said, just a bit too gleefully.

Without a backwards glance, Julianne walked off. She crossed the yard again, nodding curtly to another guard stationed nearby. As she passed, she gently pressed against the shields in his mind. It bowed.

Marcus, that man needs a rest. She passed the instruction to Marcus mentally, not wanting anyone to hear it.

Out of the corner of her eye, she saw his minuscule nod and was reassured the guard would be relieved before he became vulnerable to their prisoners.

Marcus had been one of the first people she had met who had no magic, yet could erect a decent mental shield. She still didn't understand how he had learned it, but it damn sure came in handy around here.

The New Dawn couldn't control a man who was shielded unless they could break through. Those chosen to guard them had the capacity to block them out, or in a worst-case scenario, notice their shield had been breached in time to send out a warning.

Normally, this would make mind to mind communication difficult. Julianne, however, had trained Marcus in the art of communicating with shields up.

Marcus practiced no magic himself. He couldn't read minds, or send messages outside his own head. What he could do, however, was allow Julianne through his shields enough to receive a message she pushed to his mind, or to let her read a thought in the front of his.

"Uhh… what exactly is it you do to us out here?" Jeffrey asked. His face had lost color, and he fidgeted nervously.

All he could know is that one by one, his companions had been taken out to this little shed, sometimes kicking and screaming.

They would never return.

Julianne knew the remaining 'Dawners', as she called them, had numerous theories. Most erred on the side of the missing being taken and subjected to a violent and painful end.

She let them believe that because it suited her purpose. Over time, she'd felt less and less sympathy for the brainwashed victims of Rogan. Though she had tried to give them the benefit of the doubt, each examination had proven the subject was well and truly capable of hurting people.

Apart from exposing their own debase tendencies, none of them had given her any real information on Rogan. He had used August as his intermediary and passed messages to him through Donna, a former Temple student with fiery red hair.

Rogan was like a stone in her shoe that slipped away each time she looked for it, only to dig in as soon as it was back on her foot. With only a few minds left to rummage through, Julianne had all but given up on finding out anything that would help her catch their ringleader.

"What is it you think we do, Jeffrey?" Julianne asked.

Marcus, silent and grim, shoved Jeffrey down onto a chair. He bound the man's hands behind his back, then stood to one side, arms folded across his broad chest.

"I… I don't know. The others think you're taking me out to

my execution, but you're not… are you?" Jeffrey glanced back at Marcus, and Julianne felt his fear grow.

Julianne smiled, but it was a cold gesture. Then, she slammed into his head, shredding the weak mental shield he had put in place.

Have you used your magic? she demanded, sending her mental voice booming through Jeffrey's thoughts. Her eyes glowed white.

He flinched at the sound, even though it was only in his head.

N… no. Yes. Only once, I swear. I just wanted to see where you were taking the others. I didn't see anything, I swear! His thoughts were fast and urgent, laced with fear. *Please, I don't want to die.*

Julianne ignored his lead and rummaged through his immediate memories. He hadn't lied. Apart from a single attempt to read *Marcus's* mind—not Julianne's—two weeks ago, he hadn't tapped into his power.

She hid a smile at the assumption the easy-going soldier with no apparent magic would be an easy mark. *Tell me about the New Dawn,* she sent, lacing the instruction with a magical compulsion that would make it impossible for him to resist.

For the others, she had peppered them with questions, trying to lead them to the answers she was looking for. Unfortunately, the hierarchy of the organization meant the members she had caught only had a rudimentary knowledge of the greater plan and didn't know anyone higher up except their immediate handler, August.

I was chosen. He said I was gifted. Jeffrey's mind wandered into a memory of that day. He had been visiting one of the cities to the south, looking for dyes to color the silk he would then sell at a premium.

In the memory, Jeffrey had argued over the price, haggling with the vendor and landing a substantial discount. All the while, he had kept an arm crossed over his middle. When making a business deal, showing weakness would immediately reduce leverage.

Jeffrey was missing a button, torn off during an argument at the local money lender. His skills hadn't extended quite as far as he had wanted, and he'd lost his temper. The button came off in the scuffle, and he now hid it as best he could to maintain the appearance of being a rich, successful trader.

He closed his deal with the dye merchant and turned to go, almost bumping into the man behind him. He looked up, a growl on his lips as he readied to push whoever had held him up.

August. Julianne recognized him from a memory she had seen in someone else's mind.

"My, you do have a gift for persuasion, don't you?" August whispered.

Jeffrey had blushed. "From the Goddess." He had tried to shuffle away, but August snared him in a glittering gaze.

"A man of your talent should be running this city, not slumming in it." August dropped his eyes to Jeffrey's coat, and the missing button.

Jeffrey kept his head down, wanting, *needing* August to leave him alone. Usually, tapping into this part of himself gave him what he wanted. Not this time.

August raised an eyebrow. "My friend," he said, putting an arm around Jeffrey. "I've been looking for a man of your talents. Let me buy you tea, and we can discuss it."

The memory faded and Julianne reached Jeffrey's mind to grab the conversation. August, his words dripping with a low-level beguilement spell, had insisted that Jeffrey could learn to use magic to become the man he wanted to be.

Julianne noted that what Jeffrey "wanted to be" wasn't exactly a force for good. No, he wanted money and power, gained in the easiest way possible. It was a trait he had in common with all of his colleagues.

Frustrated, Julianne forced a memory of her own into his

head. The first time she had ventured into Tahn, Jeffrey had been overseeing work in a field. He had forced a punishment onto an elderly man who couldn't keep up with the grueling demands of physical labour.

Guilt suffused Jeffrey's mind, and Julianne saw his version. August had been frustrated, doling out punishments, not just to the serfs they had enslaved, but to the New Dawn, too.

If he didn't get those damned apples harvested in time to pay the tithe, he was the one who would be writhing in pain.

Julianne didn't spare the man much sympathy. He had lain with snakes and should have expected that sooner or later, he would get bitten.

"That man was old, weak," she whispered. "You could have killed him."

"But I didn't. He lived!" Jeffrey twisted his face up to her. "He could have died, but I didn't let him!"

Julianne kicked the stool and Jeffrey tumbled to the floor. She planted a foot on his chest. "He lived because I intervened," she yelled. "You didn't even notice. Don't you *dare* give yourself a pass for not killing a man that only lived because of me."

Jeffry cringed, shame and guilt pouring from his mind so thick it was cloying. "I'm *sorry*!" he whimpered. "I'm sorry."

Marcus hauled him onto his seat, not bothering to wipe his snot-covered face.

"That's nice," Julianne said evenly. All trace of her rage was gone, swallowed by the effortless control she had honed for years. "At least you have *some* kind of conscience. I can't tell you how many of your friends couldn't get far enough past not wanting to die to actually apologize for what they'd done."

Jeffrey shook, too scared to look her in the eye. "Just kill me." His voice trembled. "I know I deserve it. I'm as much of a rat bastard as the rest of them. Just... please, don't make it hurt too much?"

Julianne stepped back. "I'm not going to kill you."

"You're… not?"

"I didn't kill any of them, not those that survived the battle anyway. I'm not overly sorry about the lives lost that day, but I'm not a cold-blooded monster, Jeffrey. I'm not like August." She regarded him coldly, waiting for him to look up. He finally did. "That doesn't mean you go free. Not entirely."

Julianne's eyes glossed over, her irises and pupils fading back to the opaque white of a mental magician using their gift.

Your magic has changed. You can still use your talents, for good or for ill, but something broke inside you. Something snapped while you waited for your sentence.

The thoughts she forced into his head became his, her words knowledge that couldn't be ignored.

The next time you cast a spell that causes pain, you will feel that pain. The next time you make someone obey you, you will be obedient.

Anything you do to another will be reflected back upon your mind. This breaking cannot be undone. It will affect everything you do from this point on.

Julianne whispered a quiet word to seal the spell, and her eyes cleared. Though she had no power to change a person's magic, mental magic often didn't need to have a physical effect to work. Jeffrey would believe, and therefore, he would feel.

Julianne couldn't be entirely sure how long the spell would last. Back at the Temple, Selah had tasked her to try a similar spell, but a simpler version that was a bit kinder to the recipient.

For the last nine years, every time Margit touched the doorway to her room she had smelled lavender. The compulsion hadn't worn off yet, and Julianne had strengthened and refined the spell over the years. This version was a little different, formulated with help from Artemis.

This rendition was a little more complex, but Artemis had assured her it would work. She trusted him and, more importantly, trusted his research.

Aloud, she said, "If you ever wish to return to our people, a penance must be paid. You will walk there, from here. You must wear no shoes and climb no beast or wagon. Every step between the town of Tahn and the Mystic Temple will be one where your bare feet meets the earth.

Jeffrey's face fell. He didn't speak, so she continued.

"When you arrive, you will spend one hundred and twenty days in the chambers of reflection. You will speak to no one, only eat, sleep, and breathe the purpose of those rooms."

Jeffrey's body collapsed in on itself. "May I go?" he asked.

Julianne nodded, expecting him to leave immediately. Instead, he reached down to unlace his boots. "Give these to one of the townspeople. Bitch knows I've taken enough from them." Setting the shoes side by side, he walked away.

Marcus watched his retreating back. "You don't think… He's not going straight to the Temple, is he?"

Julianne nodded slowly. "You know, I think he is. Idiot."

"You disapprove?" Marcus sounded surprised.

Julianne shrugged. "I didn't say he couldn't stop to sleep and eat first. If he wants to martyr himself, that's fine, as long as he doesn't blame me when he's chewing on a remnant's leg because he was too damned stupid take something to eat."

Marcus laughed and shook his head. "You're the embodiment of pragmatism, Jules. The guy's off on an epic quest for redemption, and you've already made him a cannibal."

Julianne rolled her shoulders. The spell had taken a lot out of her. "Come on; let's go in."

Marcus trailed behind her, locking up the door to the small shed. "You think any of the others you let go will turn up at the Temple?"

Julianne shook her head. "I don't even think he will. For a guy so ready to take up arms against a village for his own gain, I'm surprised he even bothered taking his shoes off." She shrugged. "I hope he makes it, though."

Marcus wrapped an arm around her shoulders. "You know

August took their worst parts and made them all they could think of. They weren't good people, but they weren't all bad, either. I think you'll have more than one of them show up. It might just take some time."

Turning in his arms, Julianne gave Marcus a brilliant smile. "You do know how to make a girl feel better, don't you?"

He winked. "I could make you feel a lot of things, given the chance."

"You horny bastard." Julianne slapped his shoulder, but the twinkle in her eyes suggested she didn't mind his teasing. "It's all you men ever think of."

"Hey, you don't know that!"

She raised an eyebrow. "Did you know that your shields drop when you sleep?"

Marcus's jaw dropped, and he blushed a shade of vivid scarlet. "Ahh. *Fuck.*"

"That pretty much sums it up." Julianne gave him a wink of her own. Then she wriggled out of his arms and strode off towards Annie's, swaying her hips just a little more than usual as she left.

"Damned if I haven't fallen for the most incredible woman in the world." Only the wind heard Marcus's words, snatching them away before they could reach human ears.

CHAPTER SEVEN

Julianne spent most of the day in bed, sleeping off a monstrous headache. All magic had energy requirements and a permanent one like those she had cast on the insurgents didn't come cheap. Even limiting herself to one of them every few days was exhausting, though she could swear the incredible effort was getting easier each time.

When Annie knocked on the door with a cup of hot broth, the shadows were beginning to lengthen. "You missed lunch," was all she said.

"Thanks, Annie." Julianne yanked at her dress to straighten it, then patted her hair. "I'll come downstairs to drink it."

Annie nodded. "Seems you might sleep better tonight if you do."

Her advice was always sound, and delivered in a flat voice that brooked no argument. Julianne shook off the lingering sleepiness and headed down behind the woman who had taken Julianne and her friends in.

Annie was a strong woman, not prone to complaining. She did seem to appreciate having helpers around to get her small farm running again, though. When Francis and Harlon were taken by the New Dawn, she had struggled to keep up with the work.

Now, she was back to running the kitchen and her small vegetable garden. The boys had rounded up most of the pigs. They found them wandering three fields over after they had broken down a fence. The family cow had returned, milk dried up but otherwise healthy.

"I was fixing to make a potato dish, but I don't got any butter for the roux." Annie let the comment hang, too stubborn to ask for what she needed.

"I could do with a walk," Julianne said with a smile. "I'll see if old Jessop can spare us some. I saw his wife washing out a churn yesterday. What's her name again?"

Annie nodded. "That'd be Tessa. I'd be most grateful for that, Julianne."

The old woman stiffened when Julianne wrapped her in a hug, then briskly squeezed her back.

"It's no bother. I already feel better for being up and about." Julianne stretched again and realized it was the truth.

"First time you went to visit those louts, you were knocked out cold for two days. You're getting better at whatever you're doing, mark my words."

Julianne grinned. "I am. Since my mentor died, I haven't pushed myself as hard as I should. I'm getting lazy in my old age!"

Annie snorted and tossed Julianne her robe. "You be back before dark, now. The air is starting to hold a chill, and I don't want you catching cold."

"Yes, *Mother*," Julianne shot back. She flinched when Annie flicked a tea towel at her.

"Enough of that sass, young 'un."

Julianne tumbled out of the door before Annie could take another shot. Though she had never been on the end of a serious attack, she had heard Bastian yelp as the taut fabric caught him in the ass one day after he had tracked mud inside.

She couldn't blame Annie. He had made an awful mess.

"Julianne!"

She turned to see Bastian coming up the road. He waved her down, letting her know he needed to speak to her.

"Hi, Bastian. Has something happened?"

"Well, yes. Oh, no, nothing bad," Bastian said, hurrying to reassure Julianne when her face fell. "Julianne, did you know that Francis had a gift for physical magic?"

Julian started. "No, I didn't. Did he tell you that?"

"I don't think he knew himself," Bastian replied. "I was trying to teach him to shield. You know how he is—he carries that anger everywhere he goes. He was dwelling on what the New Dawn did and almost set his damn hand on fire." Bastian eyes sparkled with excitement.

"Hell." Julianne rubbed her face. "How are we going to teach a physical mage? It's bad enough that half the town seems to have an innate talent for some kind of nature magic. All this untapped magic, going to waste…"

Bastian bit his lip. "Look, this might be a dumb idea, but what would you think about setting up a school here? Like Adrien's, only—you know—not run by a giant asshole and with teachers from all the magical fields."

Julianne took a deep breath. "Bastian, I know you want to help, but right now—"

"I don't mean now! I know we have too much to do, and it's dangerous here while those nutters are wandering around. But… one day?"

Julianne touched his mind, surprised to see how passionate he felt about the idea. She hadn't pegged Bastian for a teacher, but it seemed his recent experiences had opened him to the possibility.

Julianne nodded. "Maybe. It would take a lot of work to set up, but maybe we could do… well, something."

He grinned. "Thank you, Master. When the time comes, I'll do anything you need me to. I really want to help."

Julianne was still mulling over that when she knocked on farmer Jessop's door. His wife, Tessa, called out from the back of the house. "You'll have to let yourself in!"

Julianne pushed the door open and made her way down the hall. It opened into a big kitchen, where Tessa was elbow deep in a giant pot of violet liquid.

"Sorry. May came home so excited about the festival, she couldn't stop squealing. I told her I'd make her a new dress for it; I'd been meaning to anyway. Do you know that girl has grown four inches since last summer? Four inches!" Tessa shook her head in disbelief. "So, I said to her, if I dyed the fabric, she'd need to feed the animals and milk the cow. A fair deal, don't you think?"

Julianne nodded, still trying to get her head around the rapid-fire conversation. "What festival?" was all she could come up with.

"Why, the festival of magic, of course! Danil told us all about it. We don't celebrate that kind of thing around here, but it seems like the thing to do after what you all did for us. My own dress won't be nearly as fancy, but it's May's first time at anything like this." Tessa lifted the soaking fabric and squeezed it, working the dye into the weave. "I don't want her feeling like a wallflower, not that that girl could ever pass for one."

"Danil?" Julianne narrowed her eyes. "Danil hasn't told me a damn thing about a festival."

Tessa opened her eyes wide. "After what he said about you being guest of honor, I should have known it was a surprise!" Realizing she had likely given away another secret, she slapped a hand over her mouth.

Violet droplets splattered her face, and the white apron that covered her dress. "Oh, now I've gone and done it. What a mess, and me trying to catch up with everything before the… well." She heaved a dramatic sigh.

Julianne pressed a hand to her own mouth to smother a smile.

A perfect purple hand print covered Tessa's lips. "You might want to wash that off before it stains."

Julianne gestured to the mark and Tessa started scrubbing at it with her apron. "Bitch strike me; there's a reason I try to stay out in the fields."

The door slammed open and May tumbled in, her long brown hair tousled by the wind outside. Seeing Julianne, she immediately straightened, patted her hair and dropped into a small curtsy, suddenly looking much older than her twelve years.

"Good day, Master Julianne." May turned to her mother. "Mam! What have you done to your face? No, stop rubbing, you're making it worse." She darted to the sink and grabbed a cloth, bringing it back to dab at Tessa's face.

Tessa tolerated her daughter's attention patiently, only raising one eyebrow to Julianne as May darted back to rinse the cloth. "I swear, child, sometimes I wonder if you're the mother in this relationship."

"Don't be silly, Mam. Now, have you offered Miss Julianne something to drink?"

Remembering her original reason for coming by, Julianne shook her head quickly. "Nothing to drink, thank you. I actually came by to see if you had some butter I could buy."

"Sure, we do!" Tessa went to wipe her hands on her apron, but May grabbed her arm. "I won't be taking your money, though. Think of it as a peace offering, so Danil doesn't come storming over here when he finds out I ran my mouth, ok?"

"That sounds fair," Julianne answered, trying to keep a straight face.

"I'll get it, Mam," May said. "You finish up, then wash your hands, yeah?"

Tessa grinned at her daughter. "Fine." May disappeared through the back door.

"Really, I don't think it would have stayed quiet for long," Julianne said. She tapped her head to remind Tessa why.

The woman's eyes lit up in understanding as May ran in, a small pat of butter wrapped in oiled cloth. "Here you go. Could you tell Danil the thing I said about the thing is ok, and when the other thing is done I'll let him know?"

Julianne tried her best to keep a straight face. "The thing and the thing, then the other thing. Right."

She made her farewells and hurried back to Annie's, hoping Danil would finish his classes soon and get back. She had more than a few words to say to him.

CHAPTER EIGHT

Artemis slammed into Julianne's shield again, his strike weak but irritating nonetheless. Her concentration was torn between blocking him, and attending the other tasks he had set her.

One part of her mind controlled May, moving the girl's body against her will in the slow poses of sword practice. Julianne had learned the sequences during her time with the Arcadian soldiers, and Artemis insisted they would be perfect due to the concentration required.

Beside May, a willowy tree stood tall in the middle of the room. It swayed as flowers blossomed, wilted and fell, disappearing before they hit the ground. To further complicate the illusion, a small dragon perched in the branches, occasionally rubbing its maw on the bark or flapping its wings for balance.

Julianne herself stood in the center of the school room, eyes white and hands outstretched. To any onlooker, she was dressed as a queen. Her normally brown hair was piled high in blonde tresses, offset by a crown that sparkled in a light that didn't actually exist.

Her robes were speckled with diamonds, the weight of her train held by Thom, a youngster from the village who had volunteered for Artemis's experiment. No one could see the sweat that beaded on Julianne's forehead or trailed down her back between her shoulder blades.

It was that drop, inching slowly down her skin and tickling her senses, that finally broke her concentration. The dragon and the tree flickered and vanished, and May stumbled, coming to a stop in her movements. Julianne's hair faded back to brown, and the glamorous dress dissolved, leaving her in the simple linens she always wore.

Thom's hand jerked, suddenly devoid of a weight that was never real, as much as he believed it was.

"Concentration!" Artemis barked. "You didn't run out of power, you ran out of concentration!"

Julianne glared at him. "Really? You try holding three totally different spells for twenty minutes without breaking. Hell, even do it without the sweltering heat." She fanned herself and puffed air onto her face.

Artemis snorted. "You weren't concentrating. Your shield dropped four minutes in! It's the middle of the bastard fall, how hot do you think it's going to be?"

Julianne slammed her shields up and immediately, her skin chilled. She touched her head, and frowned. "Why am I sweating?" she asked. "Mental magic can only create illusions, so why is my body reacting?"

"Basal temperature. You let your brain believe it was hot, and your physiology changed as a result."

Julianne sighed. "Artemis, you know as well as I do. Mental magic doesn't—*can't*—have a physical effect."

"I'm not disputing that, although I could, because it's not entirely correct, but in this case your theory does apply. You see, the physiological basis for body temperature..." Artemis slipped into a vacant gaze, his mouth working silently.

Julianne didn't have the energy to slip into his mind. She

snapped her fingers in front of his eyes and waited until he blinked before she spoke. "Out loud, please."

"Wasn't I already… oh. I did it again, didn't I?"

Julianne nodded patiently. Artemis sometimes dropped so far into his thoughts, he completely forgot what was going on around him.

"The human body is a strange thing. If you slice your hand, there is a physical reaction as well as a physiological one. The physical is when the skin opens, and the vessels begin to leak. Then, the body responds to the perceived damage. It heals it, makes it hurt so that you don't injure it further. Yes?"

"So… temperature is more like the healing than the cut?" Julianne tried to wrap her tired mind around the theory.

"Oh, no, it's an entirely subjective state of being. Huh. I suppose the cut is, too. If you can convince your body there is no cut, will it heal at all?"

"Artemis!" Julianne snapped, seeing where this was going. "You are not, absolutely *not* to run human experiments to find out."

"Oh? Oh. I suppose that would be rather dangerous. Not even a little one?"

"If you even think about it, you'll have to spend a week trying to figure out whether I've strung you up by your toenails or you just think I did. I can guarantee you won't like the answer."

Julianne caught his eyes and didn't let him look away until he nodded. Then, his forlorn expression dropped away.

"You could run the experiment on—" he began.

"Not a chance in hell, old timer. Not even the New Dawn deserve to be treated like medical experiments." Julianne held her hand up to ward off further argument.

Diverting Artemis from one of his projects was like trying to move a mountain. He simply couldn't grasp the ethical problems with his ideas. As far as he was concerned, if his subject said yes, there was no reason not to.

"Promise me you'll drop this one, Art?" Julianne said, softening. "For me."

He grumbled, but eventually nodded. "Fine. But I want you to keep practicing as we did today. And focus on keeping your shield up, yes?"

Julianne nodded. "Fair enough." She knew the practice would make her stronger, though how much, she couldn't know. "Artemis, is there a limit to the power someone could use? I mean, if I do this every day for the next year, will I reach a threshold or just keep getting stronger?"

Artemis shrugged. "The weaker vessels do tend to. I don't know if it will be different in your case."

Julianne narrowed her eyes, wondering if he was telling the truth. She nudged his shield, but it was solid. She wondered if she could force her way past it, but it was more of a fleeting thought and she didn't try.

"Time's up, anyway," she said instead. "I have to run. Danil is planning some kind of bloody festival, I need to shut it down before he gets people too excited about it."

"Shut it down?"

Julianne whirled to see Danil standing in the doorway of the small cottage they had turned into the magic school.

"Why would you need to do that?" he asked. "Jules, these people need something to liven them up, put a firecracker under their asses. It's not enough to tell them magic is needed, we need to show them what it can do."

Julianne pursed her lips. "You're planning to put on some kind of display?" she asked.

He grinned. "It is, after all, what I do best! Look, it won't just be about magic. The men training under Marcus are itching to show off their new skills, and the whole town wants to show you how grateful they are for what you did."

"What *we* did," Julianne corrected him.

"No, Jules. *You* led this expedition. *You're* the one they look up to around here."

"Well, I can see why they wouldn't hold you in any kind of esteem," Julianne joked. "But Danil, our food supplies are still low, and everyone is working half to death to prepare for winter. Are you sure you want to load them up with preparations for a frivolous… whatever this is?"

He reached out, putting his hands on her shoulders. "They're scared, and exhausted, and sick, and bloody tired of being scared and exhausted. One night off won't hurt, and they're already volunteering—eagerly, I might add—to help set everything up."

Julianne risked a glance over to Artemis, but he was off in his own world, counting something on his fingers while he whispered calculations to himself. May was watching them, though, hands clasped and eyes wide. "Please, Master Julianne?" she said. "It'll be so much fun!"

Faced with the wide, adoring eyes of a twelve-year-old, Julianne couldn't help but cave. "Fine. But this nonsense about me being some kind of guest of honor?" Danil blushed guiltily at that. "That stops now. Alright?"

"Damn, you drive a hard bargain. You have my word, I will not say one more thing to anyone about you being a guest of honor. I promise." He jerked his head at May and left, the young girl skipping out behind him with a wave.

It was only then that Julianne realized she hadn't asked what he'd already said about her role in the festival.

CHAPTER NINE

"Form *three*! Now *drop*! *Up*! Preseeeent *arms*!" Marcus barked the orders at his guard crew relentlessly. "Hannity, lift that bloody weapon up properly. It looks like a limp dick hanging out."

"Sorry, Sarge!" Hannity jerked his spear up so it neatly lined up with the ones on either side of him. He grinned, flicking his unruly red hair out of his eyes. "It's nice and stiff now!"

"Now, this is our last practice left before we're on display in front of the whole town." Marcus ran his eyes over the line of soldiers. "I know you're all new at this, and I know you've all been working hard. But this is our chance to show off what you've learned. And what's that?"

"Protect and serve!" The cry rang out along the line in perfect unison. "Bravery in the face of danger! *Hoorah*!"

Marcus raised his own weapon and shook it, joining in with the war cry he had taught them, one passed down through generations of fighters. "Right, boys!"

"Fuck you, Sarge!" The thin cry came from the end of the line and Marcus let out a bellow of laughter.

"Got me, Sharne. Right, boys and girls!" He waited for the response.

"That's better, Sarge." Sharne leaned forwards to see past the line of men to her left and cocked him a wink. "Now, what was it you were saying?"

"I was saying," Marcus said with a point of his weapon. "That we're going to run through our formations one last time. Then, we're going to draw up a guard roster for the night. No use having an army if they're all at the same party, am I right?"

"Yes, Sir!" The cry was loud, punctuated by the stamping of spears on the dirt.

"And I don't want anyone—not even you, *Gerard*, you pisshead—drinking if you've got a shift coming up. For those who are on last rotation, you'll have to stay sober all night."

A chorus of groans was quickly stifled by a glare. "Having said that, if you are on last shift, I'll put a tab up at Mary's for you the following night."

Mary's was the local stopover. Not quite big enough to be an inn or a bar, it functioned as both anyway. The one room Mary had to let out hadn't been hired in a decade, so the story went, and the 'tavern' she ran was really a living room with a bar in it.

Cheers replaced the groans as Marcus signaled them to begin the drill.

With a quick march, the line split into two groups, nine soldiers in each. Sharne stood at the center front of her group and a man named Carey led the second. One by one, they presented their defense and attack stances, slipping into each and moving smoothly and in unison.

Marcus watched them, occasionally pointing to a slow movement or slack posture, but overall, he was impressed.

He had spent time with the Arcadian guard, time with seasoned soldiers out in the most dangerous of places, the Madlands. There, the enemy was clever but brutal, and utterly lacking in the instincts that made people human.

They didn't feel pain, or love, or fear. They just attacked. Greed without emotional ties made them an easily fractured society, but it didn't stop them from banding together to attack a contingent of guards or a passing trade caravan.

Even with all the years of training his old contingent had gone through, these fledgling fighters were giving them a run for their money. *Well, at least in training*, he admitted to himself. They hadn't seen a real fight yet, and as much as they were itching to, Marcus hoped they wouldn't.

"Soldiers!" he yelled.

They stopped mid-movement and snapped a stiff salute, one hand to their heads, the other forming a fist over their hearts.

"That'll do, men. And woman," he hastily added. Julianne would have his balls if she found out he kept forgetting to include Sharne. "Practice is over. Go powder your faces, or whatever it is you pussies do before a festival."

"Yes, Sir!" they hollered before dissolving their lines and mingling to chat before they left.

"Looks like they're coming along."

Marcus jumped and spun around to see Julianne leaning against a fence post behind him. "Jules! I didn't see you there."

"I didn't intend for you to," she said. "I didn't want to make your soldiers nervous, so I kept hidden."

"They'll have to get over it by tomorrow," he said.

So far, each time Julianne had come by to watch the drills, the group had fallen over themselves either from nerves, or by trying to outdo each other to impress her.

"I'm sure they'll be fine," she said. "You've got a roster for tomorrow?"

"Doing that next," he explained. "Any requests?"

Julianne shook her head. "As long as your name isn't on that list, I approve."

It was Marcus's turn to groan. "Seriously? You're gonna make me go to that damn festival?"

She grinned. "Suck it up, princess. If I have to, we all do.

Besides, Danil told me you were partly responsible for this whole idea."

"I was not!" Marcus protested. "It was all him, and if I happened to be mumbling something about it being a good idea, that was just so he'd stop bloody talking about it."

"The day I believe you're innocent is the day I kiss Garrett on his left ass cheek."

"Och, Lass, that's a day I'd look forwards to!" Garrett laughed at Julianne's shocked face. "I wouldn't hold ye to it. Ye'd be picking hairs out of yer teeth for days after. Real rearick rug I got, enough to make any Craigston girl want to grab it and..." He gnashed his teeth like a dog latching onto a juicy bone.

"Bitch's britches, Garrett. You just killed my appetite for lunch." Marcus grabbed his stomach and gagged. "Anyway, esteemed Master of the Mindfully Mental Magicians, I have an appointment with this here gentleman I simply must attend. Farewell, and good day." He swept into a deep bow, and Julianne couldn't quite smother her giggle at his show.

"Fine. Just don't get into any more trouble, you lot. I don't think my poor fragile heart could handle it," Julianne said as she slid past Garrett, stifling a groan as he grabbed his left buttock, wiggled his eyebrows seductively, and winked at her.

Julianne waved as she left, her smile sliding into a thoughtful frown as she mentally checked off the list of things Danil had asked her to do. That list was surprisingly short—candles and lanterns, tables and chairs, and dyed cloth to use to decorate the town hall they were using for the celebration.

That's because I know you'd kick my ass if my bright idea caused you extra work. Danil slid the thought into her mind effortlessly, and she looked up to see him on the other side of the street.

And where are you off to? she sent back as he crossed the street to join her.

Danil's eyes were white as his mind connected with Julianne's. He carried his thin cane, which meant he had come into town alone. Without the eyes of another person to guide him, the cane would help him navigate without tripping, but she hadn't seen him use it outside of the Temple.

Catching her thoughts, he nodded. "I've gotten a hang of the town's layout; thought I'd give it a run on my own. The last thing we need if we're attacked is some kind but handsome fool bumbling about with no idea where he is."

"Still," she said as she took his arm. "You could have asked someone to come with you."

He grinned as he slid his arm away. "And where's the fun in that? Bette wagered three coins I couldn't make it in alone. Have you seen her, by the way? I'm meeting with her and Garrett."

Julianne shook her head. He couldn't see it, but she knew he was reading her thoughts anyway. She quickly passed him the snippet of her memory that showed Garrett with Marcus.

"I'll walk you there?" she suggested.

"Hell no," he said. "If Bette sees me with you, she'll think she's won."

"Fair enough," Julianne said. "I've organized everything you asked me to for the festival. Is there anything else that needs taking care of?"

"Yes," he nodded seriously. "You need to wash your hair. Seriously, you look like a scarecrow. You need to look your best tomorrow!" He winked and sauntered away, his cane tapping and scraping along the ground in front of him.

"I know you can see!" she shouted after him. A moment later, his presence disappeared from her head. "I'm so glad I warned the townspeople not to bet against him," she mused.

CHAPTER TEN

"Jules, are you ready?" Marcus called from downstairs.

"I'm still doing my hair!" she called back. Technically, Annie was doing it, weaving it into the tiny braids that Julianne had seen some of the village women wearing.

"I thought you came home to wash it yesterday?" he questioned.

"Quit bothering the girl." Annie stomped to the door, yanked it open and stuck her head out. "And keep your voice down in my house, young man."

She shut the door, firmly enough to make a point without actually slamming it. "Those men, roll out of bed and into their pants, and that's all they do of a morning. They've no idea."

"You've got that right," Julianne said.

Annie tugged at the last braid as she tied it off, then stood. "I'll fetch you a mirror."

The sliver of mirrored glass wasn't big enough for Julianne to see her whole face in, but she angled it and turned her head to see what Annie had done.

"Oh, Annie! It's just beautiful!"

"Say what you like about Tahn, but we do know how to make

a lady look like one." Annie's face wore its usual stern lines, but a corner of her mouth tweaked up in a proud smile.

"I love it!" Julianne threw her arms around the woman. Julianne wasn't one to primp and powder herself often, but this was special. Annie doing her hair in the style of the Tahn women made her feel like she had been truly accepted.

"Your robes are downstairs," Annie said stiffly as she disentangled herself from the enthusiastic embrace. "I've washed and pressed them. They're not perfect, but at least they don't look like a horse's doormat."

If it had been anyone else, Julianne would have hugged her again. The old woman cared for them with a heart of gold, but she was also stubborn. She didn't like grand gestures or lavish thanks, she just expected people to do right by each other without making a fuss about it.

"Oh, here comes the lady herself!" Marcus said as Julianne shut her door.

She could only see his feet at the bottom of the narrow stairs. As she came down to his level, his eyes widened, and he let out a low whistle. "Wow, Jules. That was worth the wait."

He tentatively put his hands on her arms and pulled her in to kiss her on the cheek, careful not to touch her simple linen dress or her carefully styled hair. "You look stunning," he murmured into her ear.

She slapped his leather breastplate. "You don't look so bad yourself, soldier." His armor had been freshly polished and his hair, usually sandy blonde and floppy, was dark with oil and combed back neatly.

"You two better be looking for somewhere else to stay tonight if you're planning shenanigans," Annie growled. "Don't want that kind of noise keeping me up until dawn."

Julianne groaned as Marcus barked a laugh. "Fair enough, Annie," he said. "We'll wait 'til morning to tell you all about it."

Annie just shook her head. "Out, you two. Don't be waiting on me; Francis is still upstairs. He'll take me down to the hall but you"—she pushed the white robe into Julianne's hands—"can't be late. Off you go!"

She shooed them out the door. Outside, Julianne's horse was saddled and ready.

"I thought we'd be walking?"

Marcus shook his head. "And get road dust on your dress after Annie went to the effort of cleaning it? I don't think so."

"You make a good point." Julianne swung up into her saddle, glad that all her dresses had divided skirts for riding. Though her position as Master often kept her inside, the journey's she had taken had often called for clothes nicer than the average riding gear.

They nudged the horses into a canter as the sun dropped below the mountains behind them. As they approached the tiny town, Julianne gasped at the tiny lanterns that lined the dirt roads.

"Danil said this was just a small gathering," Julianne said, a note of unease creeping into her voice.

"You believed him?" Marcus said with a chuckle.

Julianne sighed. "I know his intentions were good, but do you really think it's the right time for this?" She fiddled with the reins in her hand.

"If the New Dawn come back, they come back." Marcus slowed his horse to a walk as the hall came into view. The muted sounds of chatter and music leaked through the old, oak doors. "A party won't make it more or less likely, and I've made sure we have a solid watch for the night."

"I guess." Julianne pulled her horse up and carefully slid off, brushing short hairs off her robe as one of the village boys ran up to take the horse. She took a deep breath to steady herself, slipping into a light, brief meditation to calm her nerves.

"Come on," Marcus said. "It's just a bunch of people, not a horde of remnants."

Scowling at his back, Julianne wondered how someone with no mind reading talent always seemed to know what she was feeling. She pushed open the door, and light and sound spilled out from within.

Inside, the hall was filled with floating lanterns. An illusion, she quickly realized, augmented by natural light from the candelabras hanging from the rafters. Fresh straw lined the floor, giving the space an earthy smell and at one end, two men plucked at banjos as a third hummed the opening tune to one of the local ditties she had heard the farmers sing in the field.

"Jules!" Bastian waved at her from across the room, and a small smattering of applause sprang up from the people in the room.

"You go; I have to gather my troops for our demonstration," Marcus said and nudged her in Bastian's direction.

She hurried across the room, giving brief smiles to those she passed and stopping to take one woman's hand as she reached out. "Thank you, Master Julianne," the woman whispered. Her eyes were wet and her chin trembled.

Julianne whispered a word to herself. As her eyes misted over, a wave of calmness emanated around her. It suffused the old lady with warmth and clarity. She smiled and bowed her head.

Julianne pulled away, unused to being treated like a savior. When she reached Bastian and saw Danil with him, she grabbed his sleeve.

"This," she said in a low growl, "is *exceedingly* uncomfortable. Next time you set me up like this, I'll make you spend a week unable to speak without launching into a theatre song."

Danil snorted. "Can you do it anyway? I've always wanted to live in a musical."

Rolling her eyes, she turned her back on him to speak to Bastian. "What am I supposed to do tonight?" she asked. Danil hadn't been forthcoming about what he had planned.

"That's your seat." He gestured to a large wooden chair that overlooked the hall. It was decorated with flowers and ribbons.

"Bitch save me," Julianne muttered under her breath.

Bastian caught her arm before she turned to go. "All the legends about Bethany Anne, all those books we kept back at the Temple? They all made it seem like she hated the worship as much as you do."

"No bloody wonder," Julianne said.

"But," he said, face stern, "they also showed how much the people around her needed it. They needed something to believe in, someone to trust. Back then, it was their queen, their Matriarch. For these people, that's you."

"So, you're saying I should shut up and put up?" Julianne asked.

Bastian nodded.

"Fine. But it wasn't just me in that fight, remember."

"I know." Bastian's eyes flicked over to the door. "I have to go. Go sit on your fancy chair, and for Bastard's sake, try and smile?"

He ducked off to speak to Bette, and Julianne flopped into her chair. She wiggled a little, sinking into the thick, soft cushion. *At least it's kind of comfortable,* she thought to herself.

More people were pouring through the doors now, and the banjo players were in full swing. A couple of older kids took to the dance floor, showing off with quick dance steps and lots of laughter, which brought the adults in, too.

On the far side of the hall, the screech of a table being dragged along the floor caught Julianne's attention. She looked up to see Danil gesturing to a couple of men who were lining up tables down one side of the hall.

As soon as they stepped back, the food began to appear. Plates of soft cheese and fresh bread, slabs of butter scented with herbs, bowls of fresh fruit and a large tray of carved meat all appeared one by one, filling the festival hall with mouthwatering odors.

Julianne tried to stand, but a hand pressed down on her arm.

May stood beside her, shaking her head.

"You sit, Master Julianne. You've spent weeks running around after us while we fixed our homes and rebuilt our lives. Tonight, we serve you." She ducked a small curtsy, then ran off towards the laden tables.

Josie, a girl Julianne recognized as one of May's friends, brought her a glass of bubbling cider. "Here you go, Master Julianne."

Julianne took it gratefully, realizing as it touched her lips that she was parched. The sweet liquid tickled her nose, and she stifled a sneeze. Josie giggled, then ran off towards the food.

"I wasn't sure what to get you, so I just took a bit of every-thing." May held out a plate piled high with food.

Used to light meals that allowed her to keep a sharp mind, Julianne wondered if anyone would be offended if she didn't eat it all. Then again, she didn't think anyone would get through all that.

"Thanks, May," Julianne said. "Did you and Josie get some-thing to eat, too?"

"She's getting mine now," May said with a grin. "We're your waiters tonight. Anything you need, you just tell us, and we'll get it."

Josie soon returned and the girls sat cross-legged on the floor beside Julianne, despite her insistence they go find seats.

Then, a trumpet bellowed out and stifled the noise inside the hall. In the silence, someone hammered a drum with quick, heavy beats.

"Ladies and Gentlemen of Tahn. May I present, the Guardians of the Border!" Marcus called out the introduction, voice ringing through the hall.

A spot had cleared behind him, quickly filled with the rows of soldiers he had been training over the past weeks. Instead of the ratty shirts and stained pants they usually wore, they were dressed in green linens with leather and brass chest pieces.

The armor wouldn't be enough to cover them in a real fight, but it was a start. Julianne watched them hurry to form straight rows, marveling at how well Marcus had them working together already.

She quickly counted their heads—four were missing. *The other four are on watch?* She sent to Marcus.

Yes, along with six others. They volunteered so we could have enough for the show, Marcus thought.

"Soldiers! Preseeeeent arms!" Marcus snapped, voice dripping with confident authority.

With one fluid movement, the troops unslung their spears and stamped them on the ground, then pointed them forwards in a fierce grip.

"One!"

As a single unit, all the soldiers lunged forwards, thrusting their spears towards the onlookers.

"Two!"

They pulled back, standing tall, weapons pointed to the ceiling.

"Three!"

On they went through twelve different stances, each movement graceful and each pose strong and uniform. The next display was a mock fight between Sharne and Carey. They lunged and struck, their moves slow but impressive.

The fight was obviously choreographed, but the audience reacted with gasps and cheers when Sharne finally landed Carey on his back, her spear at his throat. They stood, clasping hands and raising them into the air before taking a bow.

The drums rang out again and the soldiers scattered. Julianne caught sight of Sharne, flushed and grinning by the door.

"Thank you! Now, we have a demonstration from our resident mystics. Enjoy the show!" Marcus yelled, before darting off to join his men.

CHAPTER ELEVEN

His part done, Marcus fetched a cup of cider and some bread. He slathered the loaf thick with fragrant butter and bit down before it melted.

"This ish delicioush," he mumbled to the young woman at the table.

"Anything for a brave warrior like yourself," she said, long eyelashes fluttering.

Marcus looked at her appraisingly. She wore a floating gown that buttoned over her bodice, then fell to the floor. Back in Arcadia, it would have resembled something closer to a woman's nightgown than a dress for an event, even a casual one like this.

"The people of this town are the brave ones." He coughed, trying to brush off her stare. It sat on his chest like a lead weight.

The girl licked her lips, then giggled softly. "Oh, you're so sweet, too. Is there someone waiting for you back home?" She reached for his shirt, smoothing a wrinkle near his collar that he was pretty sure didn't exist.

Marcus coughed, eyes darting around to look for an escape. "Back home? No. I mean, yes… it's complicated?"

"I like complicated," she whispered, leaning close.

Marcus took a quick step backwards, almost tripping over someone's child. "I really should be going. Over there. To sit with my, err…" *Bitch take me, Jules is gonna kill me for this.* "With my girlfriend."

The girl's eyes narrowed, a flash of anger sparking fear in Marcus's heart. This was not the kind of battle he had trained for. Then, she looked where he had pointed.

"Oh. Oh!" A hand flew to her mouth, and her eyes opened wide. "Oh, I'm so sorry, I had no idea the two of you were together!" She ducked a curtsy. "Tell Master Julianne I hope she enjoyed the breads. And, perhaps, we could forget about…" she waved her hands.

Stifling a sigh of relief, Marcus nodded. "Of course. The bread is lovely. In fact, I should take some for Julianne." He helped himself to another serving, not that he intended to share it, and walked off as quickly as he could.

"Bastard's luck is with ye tonight, friend. Ye know who that was?" Garrett appeared beside Marcus and clapped him on the shoulder.

"No?" Marcus hadn't met the girl before, though he knew most of the villagers by now.

"It's old Jefferson's lass." Garrett watched Marcus's reaction closely and dissolved into laughter as the blood drained from his face to leave two bright pink spots of color in his cheeks. "Aye, so ye know who he is?"

"I've heard rumors," was all Marcus would admit. "Do you know where Danil's gone off to?"

"Gettin' ready for his little show with Bastian, I imagine." Garrett looked around. He spotted a stool off to one side and jumped up on it, craning to see over the crowd. Even with the stool, he wasn't any taller than the revelers. "Ahh, get outta me way, ye bastards!"

"You could go sit down in the front?" Marcus suggested.

"Oh, aye. Put the wee rearick down in the front with the rest of the bairns. I'm not a fucking child, ye prick. I'm not even the shortest man in town!" Garrett glared at the cluster of people in front of him, as if hoping to bore through them with the heat of his fury.

It didn't work. Instead they pushed closer, a particularly tall woman obscuring Garrett's view even more. "Ah, fuck it. Off ta join the little fuckers down in the front, then. And if ye laugh, I'll cut yer tongue out."

Marcus raised his hands defensively, trying his hardest to keep a straight face. He didn't speak, though, knowing that if he did, he'd burst into laughter at the rearick's ire.

"Fuckin' prick. Sit with the fuckin' children, he says," Garrett muttered as he shoved his way through the crowd. Still, a smile split his face when he burst through to find a vacant spot on the floor in front of Danil and Bastian.

When two children approached, he bared his teeth and growled. Instead of crying or running away, they giggled. "Hello, Garrett," the boy said as he waved. "Can we sit with you?"

Faced with two beaming faces, Garrett melted. "Aye, I suppose. Behave yerselves, though, or I'll pull ye out by the ears."

The boy nodded, eyes wide. Garrett wondered if his words had had quite the effect he had wanted, as the boy looked almost eager to see if Garrett would follow through on his threat.

Shaking his head, the rearick settled in for the show.

"Behold! The power of the Mystical Mind!"

Garrett flinched as Danil's voice boomed out over the room and his words were punctuated by a glittering shower of sparks. The golden, shimmering flecks floated toward the floor. Before they landed, each speck exploded again, turning into tiny yellow butterflies. Garrett allowed himself a smile as the children near him giggled, skin tickled by the soft wings.

The crowd gasped and clapped as the butterflies darted up and around. Garrett craned his neck back, watching as they swirled in an undulating spiral. They drew closer until the whole swarm formed an egg-shaped ball.

Faster they flew, so fast their tiny wings were no more than a blur. The effect made the egg shape seem solid, until a moment later, it was. The giant, shining egg cracked, pieces falling to the ground. The rearick dodged a piece, then noticed that others were dissolving to nothing before they hit solid ground.

Remembering the egg above, he looked up. A serpentine infant had hatched and now lifted a sleepy head.

Light glittered off rainbow scales as it stretched its wings. Launching into the air, it let out a melodic cry. Trumpets answered the call, booming from every direction. The small dragon twisted and flung its wings wide, showering small objects into the crowd. Children screeched in excitement, picking up the small candies with glee.

"Oh, no!" A voice next to Garrett made him turn. A woman was trying to shove a finger in the mouth of a fat baby. "Spit it out, Truitt! You'll choke!"

Garrett laughed and tugged the woman's elbow to get her attention. "He won't choke. It's an illusion."

"But... I can feel them." The woman looked confused.

"Nope," said Garrett. "Ye think ye can, that's all."

As if to prove him right, the child opened his mouth. It was empty, completely free of the stickiness or stains that a hard, red candy would have left.

"Oh, how clever!"

"Aye, clever... until ye sit down to a lovely roast lunch and have it vanish when it hits yer lips," Garrett grumbled.

The woman looked confused, but he didn't explain, unwilling to admit he had fallen for that particular prank of Danil's not once, but twice.

Garrett turned from the young mother to watch the rest of the display. The dragon was gone, and Danil now stepped back to let Bastian take the stage.

If Garrett didn't know Danil so well, he wouldn't have noticed the slight sheen of sweat on his head, or the pallor to his face. He had expended a lot of effort to create those illusions and would likely suffer for it the next day.

"Friends and colleagues," Bastian said taking a bow. "I'm afraid my skill doesn't come close to rivalling that of Danil's. Instead of the glorious wonders he showed you tonight, my performance will be something much simpler, and it will rely on something we mystics are taught from the very beginning of our training: Storytelling."

A pinprick of light appeared over Bastian's head, high enough that even those in the back would be able to see. It expanded, until it was a large, round image hanging suspended in the air. It showed a scene that reminded Garrett of Arcadia, if Arcadia had been built like the ruins they had passed through in the Madlands.

It was a city, full of tall, shiny buildings that pierced the sky. One of them glittered in the sun, and Garrett recognized it. They had seen it on their journey, tipped over and crumbling away, but still somehow proud as it sparkled above the ruins below.

The image changed. Instead of a city, it showed a girl. She was strong and proud, with a firm body and perfect face. Her flawless image was only made all the more striking by her eyes. They glowed red.

"Many legends exist about our predecessor: The Matriarch, Bethany Anne, known to some as The Queen Bitch." Voices rose in the crowd and Garrett saw some press hands to mouth or chest. "We know she was a warrior queen, that she forged the way to freedom for our people and saved us from a threat that our people couldn't begin to imagine."

The image of Bethany Anne slid into a battle stance, then pounced. A dark, faceless figure attacked her, and she whipped out a foot, kicking it back into another that appeared. She jumped, first connecting with a figure swooping down on her from above. She fought like a godess, dispatching enemy after enemy.

"She wasn't just a warrior, though. To assume that neglects another side of her story, that of the protector."

Bethany Anne launched another kick, this time flying over the head of a blue figure huddled near the ground. Bethany Anne stood by the figure, fighting off dark ghosts that hammered down with attacks, all foiled effortlessly by Bethany Anne.

The air cleared. Bethany Anne reached out and cupped the silhouette of a face. The trembling woman raised her hands and fell to her knees in praise.

"The world she was born into was fraught with injustice, injustice that she fought and defeated. Once she had succeeded here in our world, she took her battle to the stars to fight others like her, the gods and goddesses of the skies."

The image changed again as Bethany Anne leapt into the sky, one hand tucked into her hip while the other pointed towards the stars. She flew like a powerful arrow, past the buildings and beyond the clouds. The sky darkened as the world fell away below her, and the celestial bodies in the sky grew near.

"Bethany Anne left us her greatest gift," Bastian continued. "She taught us that the weak and innocent should be protected, that good will always triumph over evil. She left this world a better place."

The image fell away. Bastian's gaze was hard as it ran over his audience. "We squandered that gift. Time and again, mankind has run itself into the ground, over and over."

A new image, one that vaguely looked like a crumbling city sprang up. Flames rose and engulfed it, leavening fresh greenery behind.

Out of the foliage, new buildings grew like trees, reaching for the sky and then crumbling again.

"And yet, thanks to Bethany Anne, and the gifts she gave us, we continue to rise. Over and over, we rise to try again, to try and live up to her ethos and make this world what it should be."

This time, the city that rose from the dirt was Arcadia. Garrett shivered as he recognized it, tall and proud. It wasn't quite a truthful image: even before the recent revolution, Arcadia had never looked so… well, clean.

"This is our time." Bastian spread his arms wide, and the image burst into a thousand butterflies that swooped into the air. "This is our time. You and me, today. We will make this the world Queen Bethany Anne dreamed of."

Silence dropped like a lead weight. A moment later, applause thundered as the watchers clapped and stomped and shouted, promising to fight until the world was truly free of evil.

CHAPTER TWELVE

When Bastian stumbled over to Garrett, he was cold and sweating. Garrett clapped his shoulder and shoved a cup of cider into his hand, which Bastian gulped down quickly.

"Steady on, brother!" Danil swept up behind him and plucked the cup out of his hand. "That's no elixir, my friend." He winked, then put the cup to his lips and drained it. "Tastes bloody good, though."

"Feeling better then, ye blind fool?" Garrett enquired. He hustled the two mystics away from the crowd that was trying to gather around them.

"Me? Oh, sure. A few minutes meditation, and I'm right as rain." He gestured to Bastian, who'd already sunk into a white-eyed stupor.

"Aye, well I'm glad I don't have ta carry ye home. Do you mind plonkers spread that tale around everywhere?"

Danil grinned. "It's no tale, my friend."

"Bullshit." Garrett thrust his chest out. "I might be a little challenged in the vertical sense, but I'm no fool. We all know Bethany Anne died hundreds of years ago. There's no bloody way ye could know how she lived."

"Records." Bastian's voice was tired, but his face had regained its color. "There are records in the Temple, piles and piles of them. Everything we've ever found while our people are on pilgrimage gets brought back. We have a small team that catalogues and stores them, and we can access them any time we like."

Danil snorted. "I wouldn't call Angry Steve and that mange-ridden cat of his a 'team'. More like a crazy old hermit and his crazier pet. The room smells like old piss, and you practically have to suck his dick to get a look inside." His eyes widened. "Wait. You didn't..."

Bastian gagged. "Oh, damn, that's disgusting. Steve is a beast of a man! I just bribed him with sardines, you idiot."

Danil's brow furrowed. "Sardines? Is that why he stinks?"

"For the cat." Bastian rolled his eyes. "Look, some of the pictures are just guesses, and I've changed the pictures I was shown since we went through the Madlands."

"Aye, I saw that shiny tower," Garrett interrupted.

"That was a bit of poetic license," Bastian admitted. "I mean, old Steve has never left the Temple, so his mental pictures weren't that great."

"Don't you lot, I don't know, read minds or somethin'?" Garrett asked irritably. "He doesn't need to see it if he saw someone who saw someone who did."

Danil nodded. "True, but memories get distorted over time. We're trained to reduce that as much as possible, but it still happens. More gets lost in the translation from person to person."

"Like that whispering game we played as bairns?" Garrett frowned, trying to understand.

"The one where you whisper a line and pass it on a dozen times, to see how it changes?" Bastian asked.

"Aye."

Danil nodded. "Pretty much. But forget all that... we have a more important mission tonight." He wrapped an arm around Garrett's shoulder and drew him close.

The rearick ran his hand along his axe and looked around worriedly. "We do at that. Don't ye worry; I've got yer back."

Danil raised an eyebrow. "You haven't got a goddamn clue what I'm talking about, do you?"

"Not a fucking clue. I've still got yer back." Garrett glared at the crowd of revelers, still looking for any sign of trouble.

"Bitch help me," Danil muttered.

"You gonna let us in on the big secret?" Bastian asked.

"There's no secret. Tonight is the night that Garrett is going to ask Bette a very important question."

"What? Hell, Garrett, I had no idea!" Bastian clapped Garrett on the shoulder roughly.

"Oy, fuck off ye bastard. That's got nothing ta do with either of ye." Garrett dropped his hand away from his weapon, but then thought better of it. He rested his fingers on the haft as if daring Danil to push the matter.

"Garrett, it's ok to be nervous." Despite the white glow in Danil's eyes, Garrett could have sworn they twinkled with mischief anyway. "All you need is a few more mugs of cider, maybe with a little extra boost." Danil drew out a small flask from his pocket and waggled it at Garrett.

"I don't need yer pansy brew. I ain't nervous, just… makin' sure I approach the situation with due care, ye withered goat testicle of a man. Besides, if I'm drunk, she'll say no outta principle." He pursed his lips and narrowed his eyes, thinking the idea over.

"You can do it!" Bastian said, grinning like a kid in a candy store. "Go on; I'm sure she'll say yes!"

Garrett straightened his shoulders. "Well, there's no reason she wouldn't, eh? Fine specimen like meself? Right." Garrett charged through the crowd, Danil and Bastian hurriedly chasing after him.

Danil... you did check that Bette is going to say yes, right? Bastian sent the thought behind a shield, unsure what Julianne would think of them using mental magic to play matchmaker between the two rearick.

Hell no. Do you know what Jules would do to me?

Shit on a stick, Danil! If he gets rejected in front of all these people, who do you think will get the snot beat out of them? Bastian halted and Danil jostled him as he passed.

Don't be an idiot. If he gets mad, I'll just siphon it off a little. At least enough that he won't completely kill us. Danil grabbed Bastian's arm and yanked him forward after the disappearing rearick.

Goddess Bethany Anne, I pray to your good graces... please don't let us be killed tonight. Oh, and please let Danil wake up with a really bad case of genital lice in the morning for putting me through this.

No need to be a limp dick about it, Danil sent back, then skidded to a halt.

Bette was standing by Julianne, who the villagers had insisted on giving space. A small clearing had formed around her chair and Garrett now stood before it.

Julianne's eyes were just fading back to their normal color as Danil and Bastian burst through the wall of people. She gave them an icy look, and Danil's heart plummeted. *She's going to fucking kill me,* he realized. When he realized she was blocking him completely, his heart almost stopped altogether.

"My fine lady," Garrett said, sweeping a low bow.

Danil's senses confirmed that the whole room's attention was on Garrett, who was now stepping up to stand toe to toe with Bette.

"I beg a boon of ye. Bette, yer the finest fighter I ever seen in me life. Ye got muscles like a hard-worked ox, and ye legs are like fat tree trunks."

Danil winced, but let him continue. Bette was nodding slowly, and Danil realized with a start that her mental shield had gotten stronger. He decided not to push his luck by trying to force past it.

He knew the rearick had strange ideas about what constituted a compliment, and hoped Garrett wasn't stupid enough to put his foot in his mouth.

"It has been me pleasure ta be travelling with ye these past months, but now, I feel it's time to... well, make our relationship clear."

Bette's eyes widened, but she didn't speak. Danil's heart had climbed back up from his boots and now sat firmly in his mouth.

"I ask... I beg of ye, face me in a battle of arms!" Garrett dropped to one knee, a beseeching look on his hairy face.

"Wait." Danil turned to Bastian. "Battle? I thought he was going to ask her out!"

"Yes!" Bette clapped in delight, and the crowded room gave a tentative cheer.

"Oh, holy mother of fucking fucks." Danil turned to Bastian. "We're well and truly fucked now."

Yes. Julianne sent the message to both mystics. *Yes, you fucking are.*

CHAPTER THIRTEEN

Despite Danil's desperate protests, the two rearick soon stood at the front of the room, facing each other. Julianne ushered the watching people back to give them room.

"Are you sure you want to do this?" she asked Garrett. He nodded.

"Weapons?" Bette asked.

Garrett shook his head. "I'd rather do it by hand, if ye don't mind."

Bette nodded and pulled a sword from her belt, tossing it to the ground behind her. She slid a knife from her boot, and slipped another from the back of her shirt somehow.

Finally, Bette slipped one hand into the tight roll of her hair and shook it free. Garrett's eyes widened when he saw the slim stiletto dagger that had come with it. That, too, was discarded.

He coughed when her belt was removed. "No knives there?" he asked.

"What? No, just a garrotte." She chuckled at the look on his face. "It's ok. I think I have them all now."

"Right, then." He undid his belt and tossed it to the side with his axe. The only other weapon he had brought was a boot knife, and he flicked it away, eager to begin.

"Are there rules?" Julianne asked, watching the display.

"Aye," Bette said. "No weapons, now that's been agreed. We fight until one of us is incapacitated, or taps out. If it's the latter, it's best outta three." She twisted a smile at Garrett. "We won't need three."

"Very well," Julianne said. "Begin."

The simple word sent a hush over the crowd. Bette and Garrett stood, knees pliant and hands slightly raised, each waiting for the other to attack.

Julianne's eyes shone white as she slipped into Garrett's mind. Bette had quietly asked her to watch him, make sure he wasn't holding back at all. Julianne agreed, knowing the result of this fight would change the dynamic between them, no matter who won.

It would be a good change, as long as the fight was honest. Julianne noted the adrenaline sharpened Garrett's mind, and she felt his blood explode with energy as he attacked.

Garrett leapt forwards, past Bette's quick sidestep. Without pausing, he rolled on the floor and spun, kicking out a leg that she easily jumped.

Bette swung a fist down at Garrett's head and he dodged, trying to grab her arm. She was too quick, and once again they faced off. They were both flushed and grinning.

Bette took a short step forwards. Then, she spun a kick out. Garrett jumped back, then swung his fist as she came to a stop. Bette *whoofed* out a breath as it connected, but managed to snatch his arm and jerk him over her shoulder and onto the ground.

She jumped, driving towards the ground elbow-first. He rolled, but too slow and caught the point in his calf. Garrett yelped, then kicked at her head.

He missed, but the distraction was enough to let him scurry away and limp to his feet. "Ye warmed up, now?" he asked.

"Aye," she said with a terrifying grin. "Let's show these over-grown lumps how real fightin's done."

The words were barely out of her mouth before she ran at him, jumping at the last moment to angle her feet into a kick.

Garrett raised his arms to block. Her feet planted on his thick muscles, using his block as a springboard as she backflipped. Garrett lashed out with a kick of his own, and Bette flung her body back until her head almost touched the ground, feet still planted solidly on the floor.

She twisted as she came up, then drove her shoulder into Garrett's midsection. She lifted him and dumped him back, but he rolled, only just saving his head from contacting the hard-wood below.

Bette threw a fist. Garrett didn't block it, taking the punch to his gut, and he smashed his fists together over her ears.

They fought in silence, punches and kicks were blocked or parried, or withstood with quiet grunts. Julianne marveled at Garrett's quickness, his instinctive movements that barely regis-tered as thought.

Then, it happened. Bette caught a punch thrown at her face, pulled Garrett's arm down, kicked his foot out from under him, and kneed him in the face.

Julianne heard the crunch even as she felt it through her connection with him. Tempted as she was to pull away, she didn't. She had to be sure.

Head reeling, Garrett tried to drop back into a defensive stance, but Bette didn't let him, hammering his face with blows hard enough to make his ears ring. When she finished with a solid roundhouse kick, Julianne quickly assessed the damage, then dropped the connection.

Garrett was out cold.

There was a moment of silence as Bette prodded him to make sure he was down. When she stood up and raised her fist, the villagers went wild, screaming and shouting and showering her with applause.

"I think we have our winner!" Julianne called over the noise, raising Bette's hand in triumph.

"He flubbed it!" one of the men yelled from the back.

"No, he didn't! I was watching!" Bastian called.

Julianne smiled at him. "So was I. He fought with everything he had. Bette won fair and square."

The cheering intensified, until a groan from the floor made Julianne step back.

"How are you feeling?" she asked, quickly jumping back in his head. She checked his mind for damage and, as she expected, found none. Rearick physiology didn't just cause a height difference. Their bones were stronger, especially the skull.

"I feel like I've been kicked in the head by a horse—by a strong and beautiful woman," he quickly amended, seeing Bette looking down at him.

"Bloody good fight," she said.

"Aye." He took her hand and Bette hoisted him to his feet. "Damn, woman, ye pack a punch. And a kick, too."

"Are you ok, Garrett?" Danil asked. "Because if you are, I'm going to hit you myself. What the hell was that?"

"What was what?" Garrett squinted at Danil.

"I thought you were going to ask Bette..." Danil looked at Bette, who was listening intently. "Uhh, something else. Who asks a woman to brawl?"

"What, ye think a woman is too precious to kick yer ass?" Bette asked menacingly.

Danil took an involuntary step back. "No! No. Definitely not. Woman are great at brawling, really."

Garrett erupted into laughter. "Good man, ye've got the right idea. Never tell a woman she can't fight, or ye'll get the snot knocked out of ye in a hot minute."

"It must be a rearick thing," Bastian said. "I can't imagine any Arcadian lady who'd go toe to toe in a fist fight."

"Ah, the lad hasn't met our Hannah, then?" Garrett looked to Julianne for confirmation.

Hannah, the leader of the Arcadian revolution some months back, was a lot like Bette, Julianne realized. "No, he was tucked up safe with the other initiates then." Hannah wasn't just the strongest magician Julianne had seen, though her mental magic could do with some more practice.

Hannah was street-smart and could fight like... well, like a rearick. Living on the streets in a slum, under the oppressive rule of nobles like Adrien would either make you or break you. It was definitely Hannah's making.

"Bette has spoken to me about it, a little. She's been waiting for Garrett to finally work up the balls to ask her to duel."

"You knew this would happen?" Danil asked, wondering if it was too early to feel relieved.

Julianne nodded. "It's a tradition amongst the men, mostly, to establish hierarchy. In most cases, position in a team is determined by seniority and competence, but sometimes there are disputes."

"So, they settle it with a cage match." Danil's voice was flat, and he said it as a statement, not a question. He was beginning to wonder if he'd been played.

"We're not animals, Danil. Who'd wanna fight in a cage, anyway?" Bette chucked him over the shoulder, a friendly jab that made him wince nonetheless.

"So, if this fight was always going to happen, I'm off the hook for instigating it?"

Julianne regarded him coolly. Still shielded, face calm, she didn't answer until his face had paled. Then, she burst out laughing. "I think I'll let you off, this time. But for Bitch's sake, don't get involved with things without asking questions first, ok? You'll get a reputation for being a literal blind fool if you're not careful."

"Ha fucking ha. I'm going to get a drink."

Danil stomped off, planning to get well and truly shitfaced before the evening was over. Now that the entertainment was at an end, people were starting to go home and the number of children running around had dropped noticeably.

Just as well, Danil thought as he caught the words to a scandalous ditty the banjo players were singing.

"…and just as her dress flipped o'er her head
And her lover fell flat on the prostitute's bed
Only then did his wife throw the door open wide
And drag him downstairs by the hair on his hide…"

Sitting back on a bench, eyes closed, Danil didn't bother to rouse when Bastian and Garrett came to sit next to him. He could see just as well with them shut anyway.

"Thank ye for settin' me on the straight, Danil. No better feeling than this."

"No better feeling than getting the snot kicked out of you?" Danil asked, bemused.

"Aye. Now, she knows I respect her and I know she respects me slightly less. As it should be." Garrett took a long pull of his drink. "Did I ever tell ye about a lass—"

The doors to the hall burst open, and through his mental vision, Danil saw Marcus with one of his soldiers. He looked pissed.

CHAPTER FOURTEEN

"Julianne!" At Marcus's urgent yell, Danil's eyes shot open. He reached the soldier a moment after his Master did.

"Which gate?" Julianne asked, and Danil realized she had already read the emergency from Marcus's thoughts.

Rather than plough through an untrained mind looking for details, Danil went straight to Julianne.

A small army, headed for the town. They're threatening our guards, asking for the mayor. Something about taxes, but there's too much shouting to know more.

Julianne sent the information with words, filling in the blanks with quick images and sounds. Danil picked out one man who seemed to be leading the group, dressed in polished silver armor and decked in ribbons and finery.

"He looks like a right prick," Danil muttered.

Marcus, used to the silent exchange of information, laughed. "That he does, one with a right sharp stick up his ass."

"Come on," Julianne said. "Let's go find out what he wants. Bastian, Garrett, stay here and make sure no one follows us. I don't want this getting out of hand."

Since the town's enslavement and consequent liberation from

the New Dawn, Tahn had no elected officials. The townspeople had been working together so well, no one had even thought about replacing the deceased mayor.

Julianne kicked herself for not seeing to it earlier, but figured that, as the evening's 'guest of honor', she may as well earn her keep. Besides, after all they had been through, the last thing these people needed was another headache.

Making their way to the eastern road into town, Julianne soon saw the commotion. The soldiers were riled up, and she could feel the tension in the air. If someone didn't diffuse this situation, it would get ugly, fast.

Danil, calm them. She sent the message silently, on the hopefully small chance that the newcomers had a mystic with them.

Her shoulders dropped as anger and fear was sucked out of the air. Not too much—Danil left them enough unease to keep them on edge, alert for danger—but enough that a wrong word shouldn't start a war.

She picked out their leader simply by seeking the arrogance that leaked out of him. Determined not to give him the upper hand, she strode directly up to him, head high. Even looking up at him astride a stunning horse, she managed to tilt her head back enough that she was looking down her nose.

"Is there a problem?" The man was probably a noble, but as Master of the Mystic Temple, Julianne held a rank at least equal to his, if not higher.

He sneered down at her. "You're the leader of this pathetic rabble? Control your men. If they act like whimpering dogs, they'll be bitten by my wolves."

The men behind Julianne bristled, and she felt for Danil. Controlling the emotions of a crowd this worked up wasn't easy, but she didn't want to distract herself by helping him.

"These are the men of Tahn. They are their own people; I am just an emissary from across the Madlands."

"I thought as much." The man spat on the ground. "You look

too clean to be from this shithole. Name's George. Of course, that's my father's name, too. I'm George the Third." He leaned forwards with an outstretched hand. Julianne didn't need magic to know he was looking straight down her top.

She didn't react, ignoring his hand and looking at his men. Her eyes misted over for the briefest second; then, as she altered her appearance just the tiniest bit, they turned her regular shade of green.

It was an old trick the mystics often used in public, though it was of little use amongst themselves. Covering their white eyes made outsiders more at ease, letting them think the mystic wasn't using magic at all.

It was a practice Julianne avoided on principle. She didn't like hiding her powers out of courtesy, but right now, it was all she could do not to kick this man in the teeth. *Hiding my eyes is about as courteous as this meeting will get, I suspect,* she thought to herself.

"What is your business with Tahn?" she asked.

She already knew—she had pushed past his surprisingly strong shield to read his mind, and knew someone had sent him to investigate the area and see what had happened to the New Dawn stationed here.

The figure that gave his orders was blurred out in his mind, along with any more specific compulsions. Julianne's hackles were raised, but she steadied her heart rate with careful breaths to cover her revulsion.

Dropping his hand with a scowl, George looked her up and down.

"You speak for them, do you?" he asked.

"I do."

"Well, you should know your crappy little host town owes fealty to Muir, and its lord. That lord would be my father, by the way." He cocked an eyebrow, and Julianne caught a fleeting expectation that she would be impressed. "George the Second?"

She stifled a snort. Nothing about this little shit kicker was impressive. "You're here to collect taxes?" she asked, catching onto his cover story.

George Junior's mind raced as he realized he could not only complete the job he was asked to do, but fill his pockets, too. "Yes. They're late, by a month."

"And these taxes are for?" Julianne raised a bored eyebrow.

"What all taxes are for." George's irritation showed as he sucked at a tooth. When Julianne motioned for him to continue, he added, "You know… roads, protection, schools. Those things don't pay for themselves."

"Oh! So, you're here to pave the roads and build a school for the hardworking people of Tahn? Because you've sure as hell done a piss-poor job of protecting them." A few cries of agreement went up from the Tahn soldiers.

George reddened. "The people of this shit-hole town couldn't muster up the brains to make a school worth it. And why would we pave the roads? Not like the place will be any cleaner. It might stifle the dust, but the place is full of lice."

"We've spent the last two seasons enslaved by a bunch of mind-fuckers," one of the men behind Julianne called out. "Where were your fancy soldiers then, aye? Off sucking their mamas' teats? They sure as fuck weren't *protecting* anyone."

She narrowed her eyes, waiting to see if the little pustule had an answer for that. She couldn't read it before he spoke. He didn't think much before opening his mouth.

"Maybe you were better off, then," he said. Julianne's anger rose. "At least the tithes were coming through."

She pushed harder, rifling through his memories. The man was too stupid to sense it. He was speaking the truth. Cart after cart, laden with the best produce of Tahn, had flooded in over recent months.

Why? His mind had so many blank spots she was surprised he could still function. The answer to the shipments was hidden in one of them, she was sure.

When the lordling touched his temple and squinted, she pulled back. Anyone with a sensitivity to mental magic would feel a buzzing sensation in the temples and forehead when being mind-read, and she cursed her luck that he was one of them.

"If you have time for festivities, you clearly have time for work. Pay the money owed by week's end. If your little town is too piss poor to make tithe, you can make it up with fine women and serving girls. No ugly bitches—only the best. We'll take them by force if we need to."

George spat again, but this time, he missed the ground. A stringy dollop of phlegm hung from his shoe. One of the villagers laughed, and more than one of George's men had lips tightly pressed together.

"Shut *up!*" he yelled. He tried to kick the stringy goop off, but only managed to swing it up onto the hem of his pants. Letting out a growl of rage, he shoved his foot along his stirrup, trying to wipe it away. The horse, taking his motion as a cue to bolt, darted forwards. It wasn't just the villagers laughing now.

George sawed on the reins, and almost toppled off as his horse reared. "You fucking *peasants!*" he screeched, face crimson. A fat vein throbbed at his neck. "My father's army will burn your shithole town to the Bitch-damned ground!"

A quick touch on two of his soldiers' minds showed that was false. Julianne read them easily. The main thought on both minds was a frustration they were out here at all. This group of soldiers was employed by the city—a mission like this one should have been handled by the young lord's personal guard.

Beyond that, they were bored, embarrassed by their dick of a temporary leader, and uncomfortable with the presence of George Senior's new advisor. They were aware he had suggested this trip, but didn't know why, or why this unit was sent instead of the other.

Come to think of it, Julianne realized, *they don't even know what this new advisor looks like. How strange.*

One of them was already thinking of the hot dinner and warm bed that waited for him at home. An errant thought about how George the Third would spend his homecoming gave Julianne an idea.

She deftly entered George's mind again. *When you're fucking your prostitute tomorrow night, tell her everything you did when you got back.* She put the suggestion in his mind with a weighty compulsion, then added, *and from now on, pay her triple for her time.*

One of George's men gave his stallion a sly jab in the buttock and, already unsettled and probably relishing some revenge on his inept rider, it took off. The young noble gave up trying to control the beast and let it have its head, forcing his companions to catch up.

A few of them shot sympathetic looks to the townsfolk before turning their horses to trot back the way they came, seemingly unworried about keeping pace with the now-galloping horse at their lead.

"Well, that's one for the books," Marcus said. He pushed a hand under his helmet to rub his head. "What a prick."

"It's his prick that'll get us to the bottom of this," Julianne said. "Danil, you read the soldiers?"

Generally, the strongest mystic in a party would read the mind of the most important person present. This time, that meant Julianne was pushing on George. It automatically fell to Danil to examine the other minds surrounding him.

"They support him out of loyalty to his father, who they think is an honorable leader. They think the little dipshit needs a good thrashing. But, they wouldn't commit treason against their lord, no matter how much of a dick they think his son is." Danil spoke out loud for Marcus's benefit. "Jules, something is going on in their city. I bet it's the New Dawn."

"Oh, it's them alright," she said. "Phlegm face is a sensitive, so I didn't push too hard. His mind is patchy, too."

"Drugs?" Danil asked. Opiate use could cause a mind to resemble a block of holey cheese.

"Could be, but I'd wager it's too much magic. If he's a sensitive, and they're shoving compulsions and false memories onto him, it could cause similar damage."

Marcus watched the exchange. "So, what now? If he came back with an actual army, we wouldn't stand a chance."

"We take the fight to the source," Julianne said, thinking about the strange advisor nobody liked, but no one remembered ever seeing. "I'll go to Muir. I'll bet you any money Rogan is there. If I can take him out and neutralize the threat, you won't have to worry."

"Hate to state the obvious, Jules, but what if you fail?" Danil looked at the villagers. They were dressed like soldiers, but had never fought, not really. Even now, he could see they were shaken.

Julianne gestured at them. "That's why we have a backup plan. You and Garrett can train our people. Run simulations, make them as real as possible so we don't have anyone shitting their pants if the fight comes here."

Marcus raised a hand. "If Garrett's training my troops, I hope to hell that means I'm going with you."

Julianne nodded. "You said you were dying to take me out to dinner in the big city. Now's your chance." She winked at him as a grin lit up her face.

"Wait, he said what?" Danil squeaked. "You've got some balls, Marcus. Last guy that said something like that to her spent the next week believing he was a horny chihuahua."

Marcus winced. "I hope you're joking. Don't tell me if you're not."

CHAPTER FIFTEEN

Julianne called a crisis meeting at Annie's. Bastian and the rearick had already gone to bed, but quickly roused when Julianne sent them strong mental nudges. She let Harlon sleep, but Francis appeared at the dining hall when he heard the noise.

Annie set a fresh pot of tea on the table. "Listen, I don't mind you using my house to host your discussions, but my old bones are tired. You want a waitress for your meeting, you have it at a decent hour, you hear?"

Julianne jumped up from the table and gave her a hug. "Go to bed, Annie. You've been so much help, we wouldn't think of asking more of you. If there's anything you need to know in the morning, we'll fill you in."

Annie huffed out a breath and patted Julianne's arm. "And you've done much for us. Seems you're still doing. I appreciate that."

She waved them a goodnight and traipsed upstairs.

"What's happened?" Bette asked.

Julianne and Marcus gave a quick explanation.

"Ye want me to mold those snot-nosed saplings into real fighters?" Garrett asked. "Maybe if ye gave me a year or six..."

"We don't have that long," Julianne said. "But don't worry. I was going to ask Bette, anyway."

Garrett shot to his feet. "I'll have them battle ready in a week, Bitch help me."

"Ye couldn't do it in yer lifetime. Takes a warrior to train a warrior," Bette piped up.

"And I suppose ye could do it better?" Garrett asked.

"I think it'll go faster if you work together," Julianne said, letting a hint of iron enter her voice. *Bitch help me, I thought that damn fight would make them less competitive, not more, she* thought.

"I can help, too," Danil said. Garrett scoffed, but Danil explained. "I can give you illusions for them to fight. They can hit as hard as they want, no need to worry about bruising a friend. The illusions will bleed, though. Exploding heads, spilled intestines, I can do the lot. Get them over the squeamishness real fast."

"That's brilliant!" Bette exclaimed. "Oh, and if they chop a head off, can ye make it all squirty?"

Danil looked at her in alarm. "Cripes, Bette, you sound like you'll enjoy the show!"

"Just wanna make sure my men can handle a wee bit of blood, is all," she said with a grin. Garrett just watched, jaw slack.

"Bastian," Julianne said. "I want you on teaching, as many hours as you can rope people in. See if Artemis will help, too. He promised to take some children's classes, but I've only seen him do the one. We need as many villagers as possible to be able to shield."

"Yes, Master," he said. "I might be able to come up with some kind of deal with old Artie." Bastian didn't elaborate, but Julianne didn't have time to ask, so she let it be.

"So, where are you going?" Bastian asked. "Off to Muir, I'm guessing."

Julianne nodded. "Marcus's shields are damn near impenetrable now. He'll blend in better than the two of you"—she pointed at her fellow mystics—"and I know he can fight like a demon if we get into trouble."

"You're up against mystics, though, Master. Are you sure it'll be safe?"

"We're just going on reconnaissance. If there's a chance I can take Rogan down cleanly, I will, but I won't do anything stupid. If I need you, I'll send word."

"Depending on the situation, we might be able to petition the local lord for help," Marcus added. "If his men still think highly of him, maybe they haven't gotten to him yet."

"That'll be our first task," Julianne said. "We need to know how deep the rot is, and how far it's spread."

She rubbed her head. "We'll have to leave first light. I don't want them getting the jump on us."

"We should get some sleep then," Marcus suggested with a wink.

"Not in her room, yer not," Bette retorted.

Marcus stuck his tongue out at the rearick as he stood. "I'll be here at sunrise with the horses. Be ready."

Julianne pushed back her chair and rubbed her eyes. "Marcus is right, which proves miracles do happen. We all need sleep."

The room quickly emptied, leaving Julianne to stack the teacups. A clink startled her, and she looked up to see Francis helping.

"I guess you lot have it all organized, then?" he said quietly. "You probably don't need my help, but it's there if you need it."

Julianne put a hand on his arm. She knew the man had been hurting in silence for a long time, now. If only they'd had the time to deal with the deeper wounds this town had suffered before having to rush off to rescue it again.

"Francis, all our big plans could all come to naught. For all we know, that fat jerk is on his way back now. We need every bit of help we can get."

Francis brightened a little. "If there's something I can do, tell me."

"You were a builder before, weren't you?" she asked.

Few of the villagers had returned to their old professions, instead roped into farming and rebuilding the town. Francis had spent most of his time doing repairs and mending fences, in between his classes with Marcus and Danil.

He nodded. "Not much call for it here. Mostly did fences and barns."

Julianne grinned. "That's perfect. I want you in charge of fortifying the main thoroughfares. Wall off as much of the exposed routes into the town as you can and make sure those bastards can't just ride on in."

"Thank you, Master." Francis shook her hand roughly. "You can rely on me."

"I have no doubt." Julianne's heart lifted as a sense of purpose infused Francis.

His posture straightened, and he pushed his shoulders back, lifting his head to look her in the eye for only the second time since they had met.

The first time was the day he had sworn to burn the New Dawn to the ground if it killed him.

It was in their first interview. Julianne had met with the man to probe his mind and make sure he wasn't still trapped by the New Dawn's mind control, and that he hadn't followed them willingly.

What she found was blind rage and a thirst for revenge. The Dawn had taken his wife. Danielle was ill when they came into town, and was preparing to leave to seek medical help in Muir. They used mental control to fool her into thinking the strange lump in her throat was gone.

When Francis questioned it, they did the same to him. The lump grew, though Danielle couldn't feel it and Francis couldn't see it. Even when she choked on her food, or gasped for breath, it never occurred to them that it was the growth, getting worse as it went untreated.

Danielle had died a few days after Julianne freed Tahn. Francis hadn't even known. They had told him she was off to serve at the feet of Master August and his superiors, and the bastards had mind-fucked him so badly he was proud of her.

Julianne listened to him talk for hours. About the niggling feeling something wasn't right, the constant anxiety and night-mares about his wife's safety. He drowned himself in guilt, convinced he could have—should have—known better.

It had taken some time for Julianne to make him understand he had done everything he could. It was August himself that planted the first seeds of mind control, and he seemed to be the strongest of the mystics in town.

A simple village man, with no training or expertise, hadn't had a Bitch-damned chance against him.

Remembering his vow, Julianne touched Francis on the arm. His muscle was tight, vibrating with tension. "Francis, you're a part of this. What you do over the next few days, even if they don't come here, will help."

He nodded. "I can't thank you enough. For... you know. Everything." He cleared the gruffness from his voice. "I'd best be off to bed. Goodnight, Master Julianne."

Julianne waited until he had disappeared into the shadows before slipping upstairs. After pausing a moment to make sure all was quiet, she opened a door, then closed it behind her.

"Bah. I should've known you'd notice," Annie said. She sat in a rocker, swaying gently back and forth with a pile of knitting in her lap.

Julianne eyed the metal grate in the wall behind the chair. It covered an air vent that led downstairs. It did, Julianne found out as she had done a mental sweep of the house late one night, offer a wonderful acoustic quality that filtered any noise from the dining room straight up to Annie's ears.

"I *suppose* I should apologize for eavesdropping," Annie said irritably. Her face didn't give any indication that it would be forthcoming, though.

Julianne shrugged. "It's your house. Your town, too. You could have stayed at the table with us."

Annie scowled and gave Julianne an "are you kidding?" kind of look. "With that rabble? Easier to sit back and listen up here, where it's quiet."

Julianne raised an eyebrow at Annie's reasoning, but didn't comment on it. "Do you think it's a sound plan?"

Annie pursed her lips, thinking. "Seems like the most dangerous place to be in this will be your boots."

"I've been through worse," Julianne said.

Annie nodded. "I'd believe that. See it in your eyes. Don't take much to put a person down, though. A moment of lost concentration. A stumble or a wrong word."

Julianne smiled. Annie wasn't so much worried, as offering a challenge.

"Did I ever tell you about my time in Arcadia?" Julianne asked. Annie shook her head and Julianne's smile turned into a grin.

"I bet I'm about to hear about it, though," Annie said grumpily. Still, she picked up her knitting and the needles began clacking away. Julianne had spent enough time with her to know this was a sign to continue.

"A little over a year ago, three men came to the Temple. They tried to start a fight; one died. We didn't want word to filter back about what had happened... so I took the dead man's place."

Barely flickering an eyebrow, Annie asked, "Who was he?"

"Stellan was one of Adrien's most trusted soldiers. He had a dozen friends and twice as many enemies. I took Stellan's place, wore a magical disguise. I had to talk like him, act like him, fight like him. I had to recognize the people he knew, people I'd never met."

"Might sound like a foolhardy act to some," Annie said softly.

Julianne nodded, acknowledging the truth in her words. "It was dangerous. One slip and I'd be dead, my entire mission over and all the people relying on me exposed. I spent months as that man."

Annie finally looked at Julianne. "And no one caught onto the fact that you were a woman?"

"Eventually, yes." A corner of Julianne's mouth turned up. "But not until she thought I'd slept with her a dozen times."

Annie barked a cackling laugh. "Oh, fine. You've made your point, girl. You just be careful out there. Much as I hate to say it, you lot have grown on me, and I'd hate to lose one of you."

Julianne stood to go. "I'm relying on you just as much as the others, Annie. This is your town. You know it better than anyone —the people, the moods, the whispers in the woods. The moment you feel something is wrong, tell my people. They'll listen."

"That they will." Annie's needles clacked again. "A good solid bunch you've got. Enough to make a girl proud."

Shining with happiness, Julianne crept out of Annie's room. She snuck into her own bed, beside a snoring Bette, and closed her eyes. A few moments later, she slept.

CHAPTER SIXTEEN

Sunrise came far too soon. Julianne rubbed sleepy grit from her eyes as Marcus gently shook her awake. "Dammit," she muttered. "I hate early mornings."

"Come on, lazy bones." Marcus spoke softly, almost drowned out by Bette's rumbling gasps.

"I'll give *you* lazy," Julianne muttered.

She rolled off the bed and quickly threw her things into a bag. She didn't need much—a nice dress, some riding clothes, and a few personal items—but she cursed herself for not seeing to it before she turned in last night.

"Are you going on a rescue mission, or a month holiday?" Marcus teased.

A hiccup from the other side of the room made Julianne wince. Bette was hard to wake accidentally, but when she did, the whole town would know about it.

"Shut up," she said softly. "Bette hates mornings more than I do."

"Too fuckin' right she does, now fuck off and let 'er fuckin' sleep!" Bette threw a pillow at the door, then pulled another over her head. Julianne was sure she heard another muttered "fuckers" from underneath.

Marcus couldn't stop a snort from escaping, even with both hands pressed to his mouth. Julianne kicked him.

"Hurry up!" She glared at him in the dark.

"I was waiting for you!" he hissed. "Got everything?"

Julianne nodded, and they went downstairs. Marcus gestured at the table by the front door, where a cloth bag sat tied with a string.

"You'd better not be asking me to take your shit as well as mine," Julianne mumbled.

Marcus grinned. "Not mine. Gift from Annie, if I'm not mistaken."

Julianne picked up the slip of paper sticking out from beneath the cloth sack. *"Travel safe, travel fast. Thank you."*

The eloquent handwriting was Annie's, for sure. "I swear, that old woman must never sleep," Julianne said quietly.

A quick peek in the bag didn't show much, but the scent of bread wafted out immediately. Marcus nudged her forwards, and she wrapped it up again.

Shivering in the crisp morning air, they saddled the horses, loaded their bags, and climbed up. "Let's hope this trip is easier than the last one," Marcus said.

"You mean the one where we all nearly died?" Julianne chuckled.

"Well, that's a bit melodramatic," he replied. "But yeah, that's the one."

"We're only going to the next town over. Francis said it's only a day and a half's ride, if we're quick." Julianne stretched and let out a giant yawn.

"Or three if we go at your pace." Marcus kicked his horse from a walk to a canter as they headed into Tahn.

The village looked like a different place. Soft streaks of early sunlight touched the tips of nearby trees, making them glow like fire. The fences they passed were strong, the fields harvested, the long weeds by the road slashed down to a manageable level.

As they drew closer, the transformation of the last few months became even more obvious. Houses were tidy, and fresh paint was obvious on more than one. Broken windows had been replaced and roofs re-thatched, while window boxes sung with bright flowers instead of withered, dead husks.

"The town's certainly coming along," Marcus remarked as they passed the town hall, still littered with decorations from the night before.

"Not so much the villagers," Julianne giggled. She pointed to a pair of legs sticking out from a rose bush.

"Ouch. Do you think we should check on him?" Marcus slowed, but Julianne didn't.

"Already did. It's Jarv, and he's fine, though I don't envy the headache he'll have when he wakes. Keep up, slowpoke."

She launched her horse into a gallop, not waiting for Marcus to catch up. Marcus yelped and kicked his own horse, chasing her through the streets.

They raced to the edge of town, where a low, stone wall marked the boundary of Tahn. Julianne let out a belly laugh as her horse leaped over the crooked gate first. As they slowed to a more moderate pace, Marcus sighed.

"Do you think they could really protect the place if it came to it?" he asked.

Julianne frowned. "I didn't think an old woman could stand up to the New Dawn like Annie did, or that a young girl like Lilly could survive on her own while the town was under their control."

Lilly had spent her days between the forest and the town, relying on her animal friends and the magical connection between them to keep her safe. At just nine years old, she had not only fed herself and kept safe, she had sabotaged the New Dawn operations on more than one occasion.

"Marcus, do you think the world is changing?" Julianne mused.

"It never stopped, did it?" Marcus's mind was, as always, shielded.

It itched at Julianne. Usually in a conversation like this, she could skim a person's thoughts—politely, of course—and get a better hold of their feelings. Marcus's block was irritatingly strong, though.

Most times, she didn't bother to push it aside. Now, with nothing better to do and little chance she would need to save her energy for an emergency, she tried. Julianne let her eyes fade to white as she bobbed along on the horse.

She nudged his shield gently, more an experimental flick than any kind of real effort to dismantle it. Immediately, she felt the shield strengthen in response.

Good, he's been practicing, she thought.

She pressed harder and again, the power that pushed back increased. She was just gearing up for an almighty shove when he spoke.

"You know, if you want to know something, you could just ask me."

Julianne jumped, startled. "You noticed?"

"Of course, I bloody noticed. You were like a bull in a china shop." Marcus slid a glance her way. "You're not the only one giving me lessons, you know."

A feather of jealousy tickled at Julianne's mood. "Danil has more important things to do than muck around with that," she said.

"Wasn't Danil." He shot her a beaming smile. "I bribed Artemis with one of Tessa's cream pies. He somehow managed to 'show' me what to look for when someone was trying to break through my shields."

Julianne bit back a sharp retort. *Bloody Artemis*, she seethed.

"Wait… you're not mad, are you?" Marcus slowed a little.

Taking a moment to center herself, Julianne thought about it. Why did it bother her so much that he had learned from someone else?

"I guess I just liked having you all to myself," she said at last. "It doesn't matter." She smiled to let him know she meant it. "I'll just have to be a bit quieter next time."

"I bet you bloody will," Marcus chuckled. "I'm gonna have to be on my guard every moment, aren't I?"

She batted innocent eyes at him. "Why is that? Something to hide?"

"Only the fact that—"

"Ssh!" Julianne held out a hand, cutting him off. She pulled her horse to a stop and looked around. "Someone is waiting for us… and they're not friends."

CHAPTER SEVENTEEN

Francis saw Julianne and Marcus leave in the early light. He had been up all night, scratching plans onto paper, scribbling them out and starting over a dozen times at least.

It had been a long time since he had built anything with meaning, and although this wall Master Julianne wanted wouldn't be pretty, it would be the best damn wall he could build. He moved from rough sketches to lists, line after line of the items he would need, with notes on who might have it and how much he would require.

"Old Jessop has an old hole digger; that'll help," he muttered. "And I can ask Mack for wire. If he doesn't have it, he'll know where I can get some."

Francis snatched up his notes in a charcoal-stained hand and tucked it in his pocket. He had work to do.

The horses were still restless from Marcus and Julianne's departure. He quickly saddled Moses, an old cart horse, and led him outside to hitch him to the only cart he had. By the time he was pounding on Jessop's door, the sun had barely peaked.

"Pipe down, pipe down!" Jessop yanked the door open and stomped out onto his porch. "The missus is still sleeping, and she'll have my balls if you wake her. I imagine you wouldn't be making a ruckus if it weren't important. What do you need?"

Tripping over his words, Francis quickly explained what had happened the night before. "Master Julianne has me in charge of the battlements."

"Battlements? We're in a village out at bumfuck nowhere, not a goddamn castle." Jessop spat over the balcony, face curious.

Francis shrugged. "Still, I need to build a wall. Can you help?"

"If it means giving those mind fuckers a good kick to the balls, I'm in." Jessop led Francis down the steps and off to a gate beside his house. "I reckon I got just what you need."

Francis followed quietly behind. He had never been a man of many words and nowadays, he just didn't see the point of idle chatter.

"Remember old Mavis's barn?"

Francis grunted a yes, but his curiosity was suddenly piqued. Mavis, when she was alive, had lived in a rambling old country house beside the nicest barn on Irth. It was made of a material that was neither wood nor metal, but solid as rock and easy to clean. It was one of the few relics in town from before the time of madness.

It was built to house at least twenty horses, or perhaps some other kind of animal that lived before the madness. The high ceiling was the right size for the animals, though, with vents to let the fresh air circulate; and doors big enough to push a carriage through.

Jessop shoved the sliding door to his own red, weathered barn. The sun was a little higher now, and caught motes of dust swirling in the air.

"You kept it?" Francis asked.

The barn was crammed to bursting with crisp white panels stacked flat, and jammed in as best they would fit. A section to one side revealed the end caps of metal posts, square in shape with odd cross pieces jutting out and making the pile look haphazard.

"That I did. Her son told me to haul it off after she died. Never told me what to do with it."

Jessop latched his fingers on the edge of a panel. It was past his head in height, and he lifted himself onto his toes to reach. With a gentle tug, it came loose and slid to the ground with a whoosh, clanging when it landed on the hard dirt.

Francis reached out and, at Jessop's nod, lifted a corner. The sheet weighed no more than thirty pounds at most. "What are you keeping it for?" Francis asked in wonder.

Jessop shrugged. "Something or other. Thought to build an extra room with it, but..." He faltered and Francis looked away.

A lot had been left undone once the New Dawn moved in. None of the townspeople blamed each other, but it didn't stop them from blaming themselves every now and then.

"Well, I guess it's good you took it," Francis said. "How will we put it up, though? I seem to recall Mavis complaining she couldn't hammer a nail through it to hang her blankets and tack."

Jessop grinned, memories pushed back to the recesses of his mind. "Easy as pie. See those posts?" Francis nodded. "Just gotta sink them in the ground and these slip right in. I still have the pulley system I used to strip it down. All we need is a few men..."

"We could have it up in a few days," Francis remarked. He rubbed a hand down the gleaming white panel, then snatched his notebook out. "How many panels would you say you have? Will the roofing panels work with the walls? And are they all the same size, or different?"

He rattled off questions as he scratched out notes in his book and jotted down what answers Jessop could give. Then, he clapped the other man on the shoulder. "Thank you, neighbor! Thank you!"

He barely spared a wave as he raced off, almost tripping over his own feet. He would need a bigger wagon to bring the panels to the town gates, and some people to help him assemble them.

Hopefully the support posts would be made of a different material, one he could drill into. If not, he supposed he could use clamps to string up some barbed fencing wire along the top.

The time saved in building the wall might allow him to work on some more elaborate defenses, but the barrier was his first priority. As he kicked his old horse and tucked his notebook safely back in his pocket, Francis smiled.

The feeling in his chest was one he had almost forgotten, one that had been absent since the day the New Dawn rolled into town. He held onto it, fanning it to life, letting it take on a shape of its own.

For the first time in a long time, Francis had hope.

CHAPTER EIGHTEEN

Julianne's eyes faded back to her normal color. "They're incapacitated," she told Marcus. "They're over in that stand of trees. Should we just leave them?"

He sighed. "Never thought I'd see the day. Oh, Jules."

"What?" Confusion wrinkled her brow.

"You. You, of all the many people I've known and trained with." He paused dramatically. "You got soft, Julianne."

"Don't be ridiculous," she said primly. "I'm simply preventing an ugly situation."

"You don't think we could have beaten them? You are soft!" Marcus shook his head.

She didn't seem moved. "Marcus, it's one thing to fight in the middle of a battle. These men are probably starving, just trying to feed their families. If it came down to a fight, one or more of them might die. Over what, a few coppers?"

Marcus laughed. "They're bandits, Jules. Nicking a few apples and a loaf of bread from the market is a far cry from highway robbery."

Julianne scowled, then let her eyes go white. "Let's see, then. The first one's name is Joff... Oh."

"Oh?" Marcus prodded her with a grin.

"Well, he's not a very nice person. Neither is Ben." She paused, then her white eyes widened and fury washed her face. "Oh, Larry, you son of a goat scrotum. You do *not* think that about a lady, especially not one who can kick your ass."

As soon as Julianne moved, Marcus slid down from his saddle. "Here, tie the horses to this tree."

Julianne did that, then pulled her walking staff out. A noise behind them made them both turn.

"Shit, Jules. You didn't tell me they were awake." Marcus yanked his magitech rifle free and turned back to face the approaching men. Two had axes and one carried a blacksmith's hammer. He had the muscles to suit it, too.

Julianne eyed the weapon, disappointed. "Come on," she teased. "If you use that big old boom stick, these men will think you're overcompensating for something."

Marcus narrowed his eyes. "Fine." He dropped it and drew a short sword instead.

"Gentleman!" Julianne called.

One, a balding man with wisps of reddish blonde hair sticking out over his eyes, gave her a slimy grin. Julianne would have guessed it was Larry, even if she hadn't already recognized him.

Redhead's mine, she sent to Marcus. He gave a slight nod to acknowledge her claim.

"Hello, lovely," Larry said. "Why don't you put that twig down and see what a *real* big stick can do." He grabbed his crotch and yanked it.

The guy's gapped teeth and filthy skin was enough to make Julianne gag. She didn't show any reaction, though.

"Now, Larry. I know you talk big, but I've seen inside your head. You know you have a tiny, limp cock. I suppose that's why you're so angry all the time."

She hit her mark. Larry didn't even bother to ask how she

even knew his name. He lunged. His friends dove in a second after, towards who they saw as the greater threat—Marcus.

Julianne whipped up her staff, catching the tip of his axe and yanking it. She didn't dislodge his grip, but it unbalanced him and his body turned a little to follow the momentum.

She flung the staff out, slapping it on his ass hard enough that she would have bet the bruise already showed.

Larry stumbled back, right into an elbow thrust at his kidney. He cried out, spinning around to fling his short blade at Julianne's head.

The weapon whistled through empty air. She kicked, connecting with his kneecap with a solid crunch. The staff came up, smashing into his jaw.

Larry dropped his stance to favor his good leg. He spat, a bloodied tooth flying at Julianne and spattering her robe with red droplets. "I'll knock you down, slut, and fuck you while your boyfriend watches."

He jabbed an uppercut with the axe, which Julianne easily knocked away. He had been expecting that, and his other hand punched into her gut.

Julianne gasped out a breath, falling back into a defensive posture. "I know what you've done. You're a monster and you know it. Rapist, murderer, abuser." She snorted a wry laugh. "All because of your tiny prick."

She slammed her staff up, catching him between the legs. His eyes crossed and he collapsed, hands again grabbing his crotch. This time, there was nothing salacious about it.

Julianne finished him off with a roundhouse swipe to the head, again splattering her robe with bits of flesh and a spray of blood.

The sound of fighting behind her caught her attention. "Haven't you finished with them yet, Marcus?" she called out.

One of the men spun and whipped his large hammer. She easily slid under it and sidestepped in to Marcus's side.

"I figured you wouldn't want me to have all the fun," Marcus said behind her.

"Hi, Joff. I'm Julianne. Would you like to surrender now, or after I cut your dick off and shove it down your throat?"

Joff snarled and swung his hammer in another clumsy move.

Julianne slammed her staff down onto the blacksmith's fingers. He snatched one hand off his weapon, but quickly grabbed it again. He swung it wide, the clumsy weapon too slow for Julianne's quick dodge.

"I appreciate it," she said as she slapped her weapon at Blacksmith's side. He caught it easily. Julianne used his support as leverage, launching herself into a kick that connected her foot with his windpipe. "That Larry was a real piece of work."

"Not just an innocent man trying to feed his family?" Marcus, his attacker already on the ground, stood back to watch Blacksmith slowly turn purple. The big man dropped to his knees, hands at his throat.

Julianne sighed. "God help any one of his victims that ended up with his child." The thought made her sick.

Ignoring the suffocating man at her feet, she nodded at Marcus's opponent. "Cormorant strike?" she asked. It was a finishing move Marcus had taught her during the revolution.

He grinned. "I've tweaked it a little. I'll show you, if you want?"

Blacksmith's eyes bulged as he gargled a thin wisp of moist air. Then, he fell to the ground, silent.

"Should we check the body?" Marcus gingerly nudged the fallen man with his boot.

"He's definitely dead," Julianne said flatly.

Marcus gave her a concerned look. It was unlike Julianne to be this matter of fact about taking a life. "He was that bad, huh?"

Finally, a glimmer of emotion showed on her face. She turned tortured eyes to him. "I don't give a damn if I've just sent that man to hell, Marcus. I just wish I could fix some of the lives he's destroyed."

Mystics held only the highest regard for human life, treating it as a sacred gift and only killing in the direst of circumstances. These men, however, had spent a lifetime destroying lives.

The brief glimpse Julianne had into his mind sickened her, made worse because she had almost left him alive, none the wiser to the evil he had spread across the land. He was a power-hungry monster, lacking in real authority.

He took it out on those around him to build himself up. Bullying men and women, forcing himself on those he wanted and was not above killing someone who sparked his ever present rage.

The only solace Julianne had from the muck that now felt etched onto her brain was the knowledge that he would never hurt anyone again.

"I suppose you want me to clean up this mess?" Marcus asked dryly.

Julianne shrugged. "I'm just a weak little girl. I couldn't *possibly* lift those big, heavy bodies." She dusted off her robes, then set to work trying to scrub out the blood with a cloth and some water from her flask.

Marcus snorted. He knew Julianne was stronger than most women and many men he knew. Despite his earlier teasing, if anyone had grown soft, it was him. His pants were just a little tighter than when they had arrived in Tahn, thanks to the villagers' generosity to their saviors.

Julianne, always rushing about from one job to the next, usually waved off the jams and cookies the residents baked for her. She helped with physical labor as much as the organization of the recovering town, and with the extra responsibility that went with being leader of the mystics.

He picked up the first body and dumped it in the bushes.

There would be no ceremony for these men, and Marcus didn't really care if they were discovered by local soldiers.

Marcus hoisted the second body over his shoulder. Julianne tucked her now-stained handkerchief away and grabbed the foot of the final man, dragging the corpse over to the bushes.

"You'll get blood all over you," she said, wrinkling her nose as Marcus dumped the second body.

"It's ok, I won't ask you to wash my shirt." He gave her a cheeky grin.

Julianne raised a cool eyebrow. "I should hope not," she said, a warning in her voice.

"I seem to remember doing quite a lot of washing clothes just a few weeks ago," he said, sliding a glance her way.

He had taken on a lot of the more menial duties for their group as Julianne and the other mystics grappled with the effects of the brainwashing by the New Dawn.

"I don't recall ever asking you to," Julianne reminded him.

"No, that's true." Marcus wasn't brave enough to push the matter further.

Garrett had, once. Raised in a patriarchal society, he was used to letting women do the cooking, cleaning and sewing, even though he had the skills to do it himself when on the road.

Julianne had caught wind of him asking Annie to wash a shirt for him. He had walked around with an itch in his ass for the next two days, inflicted by Julianne and only relieved when he begged Annie's forgiveness for—in his words—'being a lazy hog scrotum'.

As soon as he had apologized—properly, not like his first attempt made through clenched teeth and full of half-cocked excuses—the itch had disappeared. It left him in a foul enough mood that no one mentioned it to his face, but the entire village had talked of nothing but that for a week after.

"It's ok," Julianne said. "I'm not going to inflict you with imaginary worms."

Marcus almost fell out of the saddle. "Shit. You got past my shields? I didn't even notice you trying."

Julianne burst into giggles. "No. The look of terror on your face was enough to tip me off. You *were* thinking of Garrett, weren't you?"

Wincing at the memory, Marcus nodded. "I wouldn't wish that on any of my friends, but I guess he deserved it."

"He didn't tell you the whole story," Julianne said. "You know how I found out he'd tried to dump his washing on Annie?"

Marcus shook his head. He assumed she had seen it in Garrett's mind, or Annie's.

"Bette."

"You saw it in her mind?" Marcus asked. When Julianne gestured a *no*, he frowned. "I can see her unleashing her own wrath on him, but I wouldn't pick her to tattle on another rearick."

"She didn't have to." Julianne started to laugh again and slowed her horse, afraid she would lose her balance. "I heard her screaming at him from upstairs. When Annie told him to get stuffed, he went and asked Bette to do it!"

Marcus's jaw dropped. "He asked *Bette* to *wash* his *clothes*?"

"I had to intervene before she killed him. I damn near left it too late; she had his head in the water trough when I got down there."

Marcus shuddered. "Bitch's oath, what was the idiot thinking?"

Julianne shrugged. "He's all over the place with Bette. I'm glad they fought last night—it'll give them both a fresh start and maybe let Garrett work out his feelings for her."

"So, he does have them?" Danil had told him about the events leading up to Garrett's challenge.

Julianne shrugged, not willing to give away too many details of another person's private thoughts. "The whole town can see how he dotes on her, at least when he's not acting like a dipshit. The rearick are very traditional when it comes to courting."

"And Bette breaks tradition," Marcus finished. "So, Garrett doesn't know how to move forward."

"Not without getting his balls cut off," Julianne agreed. "If they can work it out, they'll be setting new traditions, changing the status quo of a whole community."

"Could make for some big changes." Marcus reached back into one of his bags and pulled out a bright, red apple. He tossed it to Julianne, who caught it easily. She sank her teeth into it and closed her eyes, savoring the taste. "A bit like when you took the throne at the Temple, I'd guess."

Julianne finished chewing, then swallowed the food. "An expert on mystic culture now, are we?"

"No, but I've seen how you react when people make assumptions about you. Especially the ones based on you being a woman. That doesn't happen without a fight or two over it in your past."

"It wasn't anything so dramatic," she said. "I mean, we don't have secret prejudices back at the Temple. We can't. And we don't harbor assumptions based on silly things like gender, because we can see perfectly well how kind, or smart, or greedy a person is."

"So, no one batted an eye when Selah chose you?"

Julianne paused. "Well, I wouldn't go that far. But most of the judgement came from outside. Adrien, not that I gave a camel's shit what he thought; the rearick didn't want to deal with me at first. And I knew my people supported Selah's choice, even though they thought a man might hold up better in the long run."

"That must have stung," Marcus said. He pulled out another apple and broke off a chunk with his teeth. It crunched loudly, and he wiped the juice from his chin.

Julianne shrugged. "It is what it is. It didn't take long before my own people, at least, accepted me as their leader."

"And a damn fine one you are, too." Marcus leaned down, letting Julianne's horse steal the apple core from his fingers. Then, he kicked his horse a bit faster. "Come on. Let's get this trip over and done with. We haven't even been gone a day, and I already miss Annie's hot breakfasts."

CHAPTER NINETEEN

Danil stepped onto the porch as the crowd on Annie's front lawn muttered and grumbled.

"Ho, neighbors!" They quieted and looked up, waiting to hear the mystic's explanation. "I know you've heard rumblings and they're true, for the most part. Yes, we've been threatened. Some dickbag from the next town over came looking for some taxes."

"Old George ain't done a damn thing to deserve 'em!" Someone called out.

Danil nodded in agreement. "That's true. Julianne has gone to settle it with Old George—it was the younger one that came busting in with a stick up his ass, but she thinks his father might have a bit more sense and compassion."

"What if he doesn't?" Jarv asked from up in the front.

"That's why I called you all here. Training will increase. We think George, either junior or senior or maybe both, has a few of those muckers on the payroll. We need to be prepared. Training schedules are on the wall, so read them before you go. If you're not learning, go practice, or help Francis build that damned fence."

Danil had already heard tales about the fence Francis had already begun to erect. In the few hours since daylight, it seemed he had made incredible progress, though Danil only had excited impressions to judge by.

"How long until that little pig-fucker comes back for his money?" Tessa asked.

Danil almost stumbled back. Whenever he had spoken to her, she had acted the lady, wailing at her husband whenever he let a curse word slip. Now, though, she looked ready for battle. Her eyes blazed with fury.

"Is it true he wanted women and girls?" she demanded.

Suddenly her rage made sense. "Do you really think we'd let that happen?" Danil asked. He sent a wave of reassurance towards her, but she only bristled more.

"Stop with the feel-good bullshit, mystic. Is my daughter in danger if she stays?"

Danil looked her in the eyes. He couldn't see, she knew that, but the gesture still mattered to him. "Tessa, I swear on my life—I will not let a single woman or child in this town get hurt. He will *not* take you, *or* your daughter. You're all safer here, under our protection."

He watched his own face through Tessa's eyes. He saw the ferociousness he felt in his breast reflected in the set of his jaw and the flare of his nostrils. He meant it. He would give his life for these people.

Tessa watched, judging his words. Then, she nodded. "Then tell us what to do."

Danil smiled. "There will be no cap on class numbers for the next few days. If you have talent, please, help with the teaching. Our first priority is to get everyone shielded. The second is to hone any innate magic that can be used in battle."

"Aye, just set Francis on 'em! He'll toast the bastards!" Mack laughed at his own joke.

"The able bodied should also see Garrett and Bette. They'll teach you to wield a weapon without cutting off your arm."

"What weapons?" Mack asked. "We're already doubling up in training."

"Ye pile of bloody wringers," Bette snapped. "Yer telling me a town full of bloody farmers can't come up with a pile of blunt sticks ta bash heads with?"

"Ye don't need a fancy point on the end of a weapon," Garrett added. "Just a bit of weight and a lotta balls."

Bette jabbed an elbow in his side. "Or a tough pussy! Ye ever seen a wee babe come to the world, ye know those things can take a beating!"

A smatter of laughter ran through the crowd as Bette rolled her eyes. "What my good friend is tryin' ta say is that anything can be a weapon. Bring what ye got to the trainin', and we'll show ye how ta make do."

"And don't pike out on the weapons classes just because yer a woman," Garrett yelled. "Sharne is the best bloody fighter in Marcus's troop. We need some bloody skirts in there to show these men how it's done!"

Bette looked at Garrett in surprise. Grinning, she leaned in to whisper in his ear. "Keep that up and ye might have to start lockin' yer door at night if ye don't want ta be interrupted."

Garrett blushed, paled, and blushed again. "But... but I don't have a door. We sleep in the stables."

"I know," she purred. Bette turned on one foot and marched away, leaving Garrett dumbstruck and frozen in place.

After a minute, Danil nudged him. "You done?" he murmured.

Garrett nodded. For some reason, his mouth wasn't working. Danil herded him off the porch and dismissed the villagers, who mingled around the lists he had posted with guard rosters, mental magic classes and fight practice.

"What happened?" Danil asked, itching to just delve into the rearick's head and see the answer for himself. He was mindful of his promise, though.

"I think… I think Bette just flirted with me."

Danil's eyes widened and he backed away, hands raised defensively. "Oh, no. No. I am *NOT* getting involved in that again." Tripping over his feet, he bolted away before Garrett could say anything else.

CHAPTER TWENTY

"Artemis, we need you." Bastian sidestepped into the doorway, blocking the old man's attempt at scurrying away. "We just don't have enough people to train the whole damn village."

"I told you, I don't like people!" Artemis snapped.

"What'll it take?" Bastian folded his arms and glared down at Artemis. With a start, Bastian realized he was taller than him. He was sure that wasn't the case when they had first met a few short months ago.

Artemis shook his fist. "You have nothing I want!"

"Oh, no?" Bastian raised an eyebrow. "I'm a mystic. One with the ear of the Master. In fact, she's already agreed to help me with a little project I think you'll find quite interesting." *Ok*, Bastian admitted to himself, safe behind a mental shield. *She said she'd think about it. Close enough, right?*

Artemis narrowed his eyes. "What kind of project."

"Oh, nothing exciting. Just a multi-modality school. Here. In Tahn."

Artemis froze. "Here?" he whispered.

"Of course, it'll take a lot to set up. We'll need loads of the regular teaching books, but also some of the more obscure scrolls and histories. I mean, we'll be breaking new ground here."

"The histories? Of the other magics?" Artemis's eyes were like saucers, shining in excitement.

"Of course, access to those records will be highly restricted." Bastian shook his head regretfully. "They simply wouldn't be shared with just anyone. Only a trained mystic who'd sacrificed themselves for the greater—"

"I'll do it!" Artemis threw his hands up in defeat. "I'll take all the bloody classes! Just promise me, you'll give me access to everything. And there won't be any more strings! I'm not letting you round me up as some kind of overrated babysitter for this play center you're starting up."

Bastian laughed at his fierce scowl. "Honestly? I don't think we'd put the students through that."

Artemis scowled even harder. "I'm the best teacher they'd get, short of the bloody Founder."

"Do we have a deal? Your help now, for access to the school library on an ongoing basis, if and when we get it set up." Bastian held his breath, hoping Artemis didn't catch the 'if' clause.

"Fine, fine. And I suppose you'll be skipping your own sessions with me?"

"Unless you can show me how to teach a physical user." Bastian turned to go, then whirled back as Artemis clicked his tongue. He only did that when he was thinking, hard. "Wait… can you?"

"It's all theory, mind," Artemis said. "And I won't take the students on myself. I can give you some pointers, though."

Bastian cried out in glee, then jerked the older man into a rough hug. "Artemis, you're the best damn asshole I've ever met."

He stayed in the stables that Artemis had made his home for another twenty minutes, hashing out the details of Artemis's new classes, and getting a basic rundown on the magic types and how they were used.

"Right. And you're sure you can't show me the hand gestures?" Bastian asked when they were done.

"Did you listen at all? The gestures are unique to the magic user. Physical mages just flop their hands about, the same way we garble gibberish when we cast." Artemis waved him off. "Go away. I want at least five minutes of peace before I wade into this shit hole of a job you've given to me."

Bastian chuckled as he left. The old man was getting grumpier by the day, and yet he refused to leave. Everyone in the damn town knew it was because he was worried about them. His tough, bristly exterior seemed to prickle most at the people he respected, or cared for most.

Julianne was the only one who seemed able to tolerate him most days, and even she had her limits.

Swinging a leg over his horse, Bastian wondered if he should wait until Artemis actually showed up at the pending class. Then, he shrugged. Artemis knew the stakes.

Bastian had no doubt he would have let himself be talked into it eventually, but the young mystic had an ulterior motive. He *did* want Artemis to form a part of the new school, if he could convince Julianne to let him help set it up.

He squashed down the fear that his idea would be taken away from him. He knew Julianne wouldn't do that. She encouraged ownership of ideas, and he knew he was technically qualified to do pretty much anything he wanted as a mystic, now that his own training was over and he had gone on his pilgrimage.

More and more, he thought of Tahn as his home. As he travelled through the city towards the gate, he was filled with pride at how far the people had come in the past weeks. They repaired months of damage to buildings and farms, and had bonded together, helping each other heal after such loss.

His heart swelled further when he saw the wall. The stark white barrier reached high enough to slow anyone, but a physical

Mage who had the power to propel themselves over it with magic.

Along the top, metal plates attached coils of barbed wire. Bastian squinted and made out thin spikes pointing up beneath the wire. Anyone who made it to the top of that wall would be in for a painful surprise.

Bastian cupped his hands to his mouth and took a deep breath. "Francis?"

"North end!" A man called back, pointing to the left.

Bastian tugged on one rein and turned his horse that way, heading down to a cluster of people and... "What in the frozen hells of the Bastard's grave is *that*?"

The 'that' he referred to was a bear. As Bastian watched, it rose on two feet to grasp a dangling rope in its mouth. Then it fell back to all fours and ambled backwards.

As the bear pulled at the rope, a huge, white, wall partition slowly lifted. Men stood on either side, guiding it into place. Within minutes, the defensive wall around the village had even extended by several feet.

"Lilly?" Bastian called, spotting the young girl watching the display.

She waved at him distractedly, not taking her eyes off the hanging wall section. "Let it go, Snuffy."

The hollow thud reverberated through the dirt below Bastian's feet as the wall slotted in, falling to the ground. The men stepped back and one leaned forwards to give it a tentative shove.

"All good, Francis. You ready for another?"

"Snuffy wants to eat, first. And he'd like to roll around in the sun. It's such a lovely day." Lilly rubbed the bear's head.

"Of course, Lilly. Tell Snuffy he has our thanks." Francis stepped out from the small circle of men warily watching the bear.

"He knows," she said. "He can smell it on you."

Francis turned his head, giving one armpit a reflexive sniff.

He wrinkled his nose, then shrugged. "You've spoken to the wolf pack? You're sure they'll dig for us tonight?"

Lilly nodded. "Just don't forget to leave out the meat. They'll have to take time away from the hunt, and they'll starve over winter if they don't get enough to eat."

"Lilly, if they can do this for us, I'll give them a whole buck every week until snowfall."

Lilly threw her arms around him and he rocked back, unbalanced. "Thank you, Francis!" She ran off to hurry Snuffy away from the wall.

Francis caught sight of Bastian and wandered over, shaking his head. "Can't say as I expected to have a beast and a little guild on my construction team, but I can't say as I'm complaining, either."

"Are you sure feeding wolves is the best idea?" Bastian asked. "I know Lilly cares for them, and she can control them to a degree, but if their population increases..." he let the statement hang.

Francis shrugged. "We've always had a great many in the forest around Tahn. Used to lose so many lambs we were ready to give up. Too scared to let the kiddies play outside, too."

"And then?" Bastian sensed a story.

"Well, Lilly came along. Kept getting a thrashing for sneaking out to the woods. She said the animals wouldn't touch her, but we didn't really understand then. Her pa took her to see the mangled corpse of a lamb they'd attacked that morning. It got tangled in a fence and they couldn't drag the body off."

"That's a bit... much. How old was she?" Bastian asked.

Francis wiggled his fingers, counting. "Five, by my guess. She was hysterical. Bit her Pa on the hand and when he let go, she bolted like a scared horse. Came back three days later, covered in dirt, lost her shoes, but happier than I've seen her. Never saw a wolf or lost an animal since."

Bastian reeled at the thought. "Five years old and she spent three nights in a forest full of wolves? Her parents must have been beside themselves."

Francis glowered. "Let's not touch on that. Don't like speaking ill of the dead."

Bastian nodded in understanding. He had heard Lilly's parents described as 'odd', but not in a way that suggested fondness. "Well, I'm glad Lilly's safe now… but I need to steal you away, my friend."

"I have a job set by the Master herself." He darted a glance back at his wall, pride etched on his face.

Bastian nodded. "I know, and I won't keep you too long. But if we can harness that power you've got, it could be invaluable in battle."

Francis chewed his lip as he thought it over. Then, he nodded. "Fair enough. I want to help in any way I can."

He turned back to direct the men he had been working with to take a break. "We'll start again at three," he instructed.

Bastian took Francis to a yard behind the town hall. An old shed stacked with hay bales made a wind break, and Bastian shrugged off his robe in the heat. He dropped it on a pile of loose straw, then gently stretched out his muscles.

He rode almost daily now, a requirement to get around the sprawling village. That didn't mean his muscles had learned to appreciate it yet.

"So, do I need to do the meditating thing again?" Francis asked dubiously. So far, he had only managed to conjure a small flame and only once.

"Do you remember what happened just before you made the fire last time?" Bastian asked.

Francis shrugged. "I was trying not to think about it. Didn't want to burn Ma's house down while I was sleeping."

Bastian chuckled. "I promise you, it won't. You can't cast accidentally. It requires concentration and focus."

Francis didn't look convinced. Still, he waited patiently for Bastian's instructions.

"Artemis says you need to make a gesture, do something with your hand. You don't remember what your fingers were doing last time?" Bastian asked.

"Nope."

Swallowing down frustration, Bastian tried another route. "Ok, we'll start with meditation. Instead of the calm, though, I want you to hold out your hand and imagine a flame."

Francis lifted his arm. Bastian waited. After a few minutes, Francis dropped his arm.

"Sorry. I can't hold it up no more." He looked defeated and they had barely begun.

"Look, Francis, I know this is hard. You're trying to do something that even I can't comprehend. You can do it, though. I saw you. We just need to figure out how."

Francis kicked at a clump of dirt. "If I don't, those bastards will hurt our town again, won't they."

Bastian grabbed his arm. "You think I'd let that happen? That any of us would? Why do you think we've been riding you so hard, pushing you through all those mind-clearing exercises and flicking your shields with imaginary stones until you're ready to punch us?"

Francis yanked his arm back, face flushed. "Do you think I'm stupid? I know we can't win, I know a few weeks of fucking about ain't gonna do squat against those people. They're not weak, or stupid. You don't think they can just walk on in here and fuck us over again in a heartbeat?"

"Francis, you've come so far—"

"Not far enough!" Francis raised a clenched fist, holding it back with an effort. Then, he spat out a growl as he opened his hand and let it fall. "I'm sorry, Bastian. I know you've tried. It's not that you failed, it's that you never had a chance in the first place." He turned to go.

"Francis, please. I—" Bastian paused. "What's that smell?"

"What?" Francis glanced back, caught by the unexpected question. Then, he jumped, eyes wide. "Fire. *FIRE!*"

Bastian spun. The pile of dry grass he had tossed his coat onto was now burning, the flames already a foot high. "What in the hell?"

He ripped off his shirt and slapped it at the flame, Francis beside him trying to stomp out the embers. When the last flickers were gone and the ash had stopped smoking, they leaned against the wall, exhausted by the rush of activity.

"If that had reached the feed shed, we'd have been in some serious trouble," Francis commented.

"Bloody stupid place to teach you to shoot fire," Bastian said. "I take the blame."

Francis laughed. "You think that was *me?*" His smile fell away as Bastian simply stood there. "It wasn't. I mean, I didn't do anything."

"The hell you didn't. You got angry, Francis." Bastian kicked himself for not realizing sooner. The first time Francis had cast a fire spell, he had been burning up inside, thinking about the New Dawn and all they had taken from him. This time, he had been thinking about what they might do next.

"That thing I did with my fist," Francis said. "You think that was the thing?"

Bastian shrugged. "It was a thing. The spell you cast this time wasn't the same as the first one. Then, the fire was in your hand. This time it was like you threw it. Not a fireball, because we'd have seen that."

"I guess I maybe did feel something. Like… a letting go. I was trying to let go of the anger, but it felt… different." Francis lifted his hands and gazed at them in wonder. "I really did that."

"Well, it didn't start itself." Bastian pinched when Francis flexed his hands. "Before you try again, maybe we should head somewhere a little less flammable. And maybe have some water buckets nearby, too."

"There's a pond in one of the fields at Ma's. The wall, though —you mind if I go back and finish? Master Julianne asked me to make sure it got done."

Bastian nodded, seeing lines of fatigue around Francis's eyes. Though it was only a tiny fire, he was far from used to creating energy like that from nothing. He would need to tread carefully, lest he burn the man out. "That's fine. I have to go see to some things anyway. We can try again at first light."

Francis nodded, then reached out a hand. Trying not to show his nervousness, Bastian shook it firmly. Francis's skin was cool and smooth, with no sign of the damage it had just done.

"Thank you, Bastian. I know we Tahn folk can be a bit ornery sometimes, but we do appreciate what you've done."

"I know, Francis. I know."

CHAPTER TWENTY-ONE

Julianne and Marcus slowed as they approached the city, dismounting as soon as the gates were in sight. Unlike Tahn, the residents of Muir were wrapped inside the high stone walls, protected by heavy iron gates that were guarded by soldiers in sparkling armor.

Julianne picked off the last of the grass that clung to her clothes. They had spent the night sleeping under the stars, opting to leave the tent rolled up so they could enjoy the last of the warm weather, and make an early start in the morning.

"Well, it seems someone is certainly profiting from the nearby towns," Marcus commented. "Not one bloody soldier seen in Tahn, and these bozos are prancing about in gear that looks like it hasn't seen a day of battle."

As much as Marcus hated Adrien, he at least had to admit that he had protected the smaller towns and estates around Arcadia well. Of course, they were mostly inhabited by Adrien's elite class of nobles.

"Steady on," Julianne said. "We don't want to get kicked out before we even get in."

"Can't you just waggle your eyebrows and hocus pocus them?" Marcus asked.

"I already have," Julianne said calmly. He looked up to see her eyes shining white. "But it'll be a lot more work with you making a ruckus. Just move slowly and quietly."

Marcus did as she asked, carefully walking his horse past the gatekeepers. The soldiers didn't show any sign of their approach and Marcus held his breath as they stepped inside.

The town was bustling with activity. Horses trod the roads, some decked out in shiny leather and brass, others ridden with worn saddles and old ropes for a harness. The ground was hard, the flop of hooves suggesting that underneath the veneer of dirt, the roads were cobbled.

"Marcus, you look like you're about to pop," Julianne giggled.

He let out a whoosh of air. "I was being quiet, like you said!" he protested. He nudged his horse down one of the wider roads through the city.

"Do you want to visit the brothel now, or later? We'll have to find a place to stay, and I need a way to speak to George Senior on the quiet, too."

"The… what?" Marcus asked, sure he had heard her wrong.

"The brothel." She arched an eyebrow. "What, scared of a few girls?"

"I… just…"

Julianne burst out laughing, gripping her saddle so she wouldn't fall off her horse. "Oh, Marcus. The look on your face is just *priceless!* I planted a suggestion in Little George's head to tell his favorite prostitute everything he knows about the New Dawn, and any action he's taken since he got back."

Marcus sagged in relief. "I thought… never mind." The pink in his cheeks made her laugh even more, causing a few passers-by to look over, frowning at the odd behavior.

"You… actually thought… I'd send you off to get serviced by

some poor girl in a sex factory, while I wait… patiently outside?" Julianne heaved breaths in between her shaking words, dissolving back into laughter as soon as she was done.

"No! I mean… Hell, Jules, give me a break." The pink was now purple and Marcus tugged at the neck of his shirt, trying desperately to cool his face.

Coughing, Julianne desperately gathered her senses and slipped into a meditation. She broke it twice, unable to suppress her mirth. Finally, she was calm.

Still, she couldn't resist one more jab. "Anyway, it's not like we've never spent time in a prostitute's room together before."

When she had been outed as a spy, posing as Stellan, a trap was laid at the local Arcadian brothel. Julianne had been frequenting it to keep up appearances, lulling the girl to sleep once she was in the room and planting false memories in her head.

"I hate you," Marcus mumbled. The color in his face hadn't subsided. "And I need a drink. I bloody well deserve one, putting up with you. I'll find the inn and you can find the bloody hooker. Don't wake me up when you come in."

Julianne pressed her lips together tightly, holding back another jab at Marcus about "waking him up when she came in." Though their relationship hadn't passed beyond a few kisses and some flirting, the tensions sometimes lay thick enough to cut with a sword.

Resolving to behave herself in case she dug a deeper hole than she was ready for, Julianne caught Marcus by the arm. He watched as her eyes flicked white for a bare moment, then cleared as she disguised them.

She stared vacantly, occasionally tipping her head a little in one direction, then another. Finally, she blinked and smiled. "Take that road. Don't stop at the first place, keep going. It's not too far."

"Bloody woman," was all Marcus said before he kicked his horse into a trot and disappeared into the throng of people and horses in the street.

CHAPTER TWENTY-TWO

Julianne regarded the clean, white building in front of her. The front door was small and unassuming, with no signage to signal what lay inside.

Not for the first time, Julianne shook her head. She wanted Marcus there with her, and wasn't happy at the idea of him running about town alone. He had never come up against the New Dawn directly, and although his innate gift for mental shields should protect him, she preferred to play it safe.

Julianne took a slow breath, slipping into a meditative state. She lowered her eyelids to hide the whiteness and centered herself. She felt the connection with the world around her.

The sun warmed her hands and face. The cobbled stones under her feet pushed hard lumps through the soft soles of her shoes. Her nose filled with the scent of horse, sweat, and sex, while her ears vaguely noted the chatter of the townspeople, the clang of a distant metal worker, hoofbeats, singing, and a loud crow.

Opening her eyes, Julianne muttered a quiet word. She stepped forwards, crossed the road and knocked loudly on the door. To anyone in the street, however, she was no longer the white-robed woman who led the mystics of the Heights.

Instead, anyone watching would see a young man with dark hair and green eyes, one who had a smug twist to his mouth and an arrogant posture.

A small peephole slid open. Brown eyes peered out, regarding the well-dressed man in fine silks and dropping to the fat purse hanging from his belt. Julianne gave the pouch a tap, and the coins inside clinked loudly.

The peephole snapped shut. A moment later, the narrow door swung open.

"Welcome to the House of Friendship, sir." The woman batted her eyelids and twitched the sheer cloth of her dress.

Julianne cocked an eyebrow, acting unimpressed. "I'm not here for friendship," she growled in a man's voice.

The girl smiled seductively. "Whatever you're here for, we can provide. That is, of course, if you can afford it."

"Oh, I can afford it." Julianne looked around the room.

Incense burned on the walls, making the room hazy. Silks hung from the ceiling, tied so that they billowed and undulated in the breeze from an upper window. The floor was green with pillows, and couches were scattered haphazardly about.

Across from her, one man lay on an ornate daybed, passed out. Another sat nearby, limply hanging onto a brass cup that leaned dangerously to one side. As Julianne turned away, it tipped just a little too far. Dark wine patterned on the carpet below.

"We're quiet at this time of day," the girl whispered. "You've got the pick of all the ladies. There are a few men out back, too, if that's what you prefer?"

Julianne quickly brought to mind the image of George's favorite girl. "Are they all as old as you?" she asked, trying not to show her distaste at the comment. She could just brainwash her way through, but acting the part instead would allow her to conserve her mental energy.

Her companion didn't seem offended. "We have plenty to choose from, my lord."

"I like the pale ones. Skin like milk, hair like fine sand." Julianne stopped short of asking for anything too specific. She didn't want to draw attention to herself.

Julianne waited patiently while the girl disappeared behind a curtain, trying to ignore the men in the room with her. A moment later, George's girl sauntered out. "Greetings, my lord."

Julianne regarded her a moment, then nodded. "You'll do."

"This way." The girl gestured to one of the curtains and Julianne followed her out, paying no attention to her swaying hips.

They went down a short hallway, past several doors. Each one had something hanging from the doorknob—a necklace, or scarf, or in one case, a shoe.

When they came to an unmarked door, the prostitute—Polly, Julianne read from her mind—pushed it open and ushered Julianne through. She peeked down the hallway before closing it, and draped a ribbon on the knob before shutting it behind them.

Polly turned around and gasped to see a small woman toe to toe with her, where the tall man should have stood. Unlike her wealthy client, this girl looked alert and dangerous. Her eyes glowed with the white heat of an over-baked coal.

Polly opened her mouth to scream. Before she could make a sound, her muscles sagged and her mouth dropped shut. Julianne led her to the bed and sat her down.

"Polly, when did Lord George last visit?" Julianne laced the words with light compulsion.

The girl wasn't particularly resistant, just a little afraid. Julianne drained a little of the fear to make her comfortable, not that she would remember a single thing when they parted ways.

"Last night," she murmured in a flat voice.

"What did he tell you about his trip to Tahn?" Julianne demanded.

She knew from experience not to ask for 'everything he said'. That would leave the poor girl compelled to repeat everything that slipped through his lips, and could take hours.

"He'd come from a mission for his father's advisor. Something about insurgents taking over the town, he wasn't really sure what had happened. He was asked to go there, and find out what happened to the people the advisor had stationed there."

So, he's referring to us as insurgents? Not surprising, Julianne thought.

Polly kept talking. "Tobias lost a horseshoe. It slowed them, and George was getting angry. He told the men to leave him behind, and they refused because of the bandits. George couldn't do anything about it. It made him so angry."

Wide eyes turned up to Julianne, devoid of empathy. "It made him feel impotent. He told me that, before he hit me." A hand drifted to her jaw and looking more closely, Julianne saw the makeup Polly had used to hide the bruise.

"He got to Tahn. Lied about his reason for being there. He thought if the townspeople paid him to go away, he could keep a cut of the money. They made him angry, though. A girl—" Understanding dawned on Polly's face, and Julianne made sure to note that this prostitute was anything but stupid.

"The girl and her friends made a fool of him. He's going to tell the advisor that the town is riddled with insurgents, that they have to lead an army there to destroy them. He has to keep it from his father, because his plan will fall apart."

"Then what?" Julianne leaned closer, urgency in her voice.

"Then he fucked me. While he did it, he talked. He told me about the advisor—he's been here for months, but George still doesn't know his name. That makes him angry, too. The patches in his memory make him wonder if he's going insane. He just kept talking and talking."

Polly told Julianne that the advisor had been playing tricks on his father, but that George Senior hadn't fallen for all of them. He couldn't say what the tricks were, just that it had happened. He told her about the new faces, slowly taking positions in the town.

Julianne dove into her head. She watched as Polly connected dots all over the place—the talk about the new advisor brought a flash of memory, a well-dressed man Polly had seen more than once. Julianne recognized him immediately.

How like a power-hungry dictator to wipe only the minds he thought mattered. George the Third and all his soldiers had all had every trace of Rogan's face removed from their memory. Not Polly. As a lowly commoner, she would have been beneath his notice.

It was Rogan. A thrill of fear and excitement went through Julianne at the thought of taking him down at last. Polly kept on with her story, telling about a red-haired woman and a sleazy little man. The first she had seen—that was Donna, of course. The second she hadn't, but Julianne guessed it was August.

Under the words, Polly was thinking about the recent absence of Lord George Senior, and how the city was slowly falling into disorder and disrepair. Their normally bright, clean city was now hit with higher taxes and fewer services, leading residents to start grumbling.

The city guard had increased. Lord George had given them directions to stamp out violence and unrest, using ruthless tactics that even some of the guards employed with reluctance.

More jobs meant not only relief for the poorer families, but more men with free coin to spend at the brothel. Polly and the other workers for Madam Rosa could barely keep up.

The problem with that was in recent weeks, rumors were flying that Lord George no longer approved of the practice. Plans were already in place to move the business to another town if the crackdown became reality.

Polly was still rattling off her story. She mentioned George had attended to his business a lot faster than usual—not that he ever took long—and left.

"He threw money on the bed, emptied his purse. He said he didn't know why he was doing it, he was confused. He still left it there, though." A smile traced Polly's lips as she thought of the sudden windfall.

"What will you do with it?" Julianne asked.

There was no compulsion behind the question, but Polly seemed happy to answer it, thanks to Julianne's emotional dampener.

"Start me own business. I've always wanted to be a madam, have me own group of girls. Madam Nacht. They say it means night in one of the old tongues."

Julianne shuddered. *It means a hell of a lot more than that,* she mused, thinking of the legend of Queen Bethany Anne's creator and companion, Michael Nacht. Though, he was said to be responsible for Bethany Anne's power, it was unsure who was stronger. Many of the legends suggested the student had overtaken the master before the world went to hell.

"Polly, how can I meet Lord George? Where would I go if I wanted to see him away from his advisors?" She wanted to mind read him.

Her first priority was calling off the attack on Tahn. She had to see how tight he was snared and if she could break any hold the New Dawn had over him.

"They're always with him. Maybe at the Cirque. They've a new performance debuting in a couple of days, he always likes to see the first showing. He'll be guarded, but not by them." She spat the last word with venom.

Julianne reached out to touch Polly's cheek. Her eyes flared white, and she murmured another word. "When I walk out that door, you will forget everything that happened in this room. You will remember the handsome young trader. He wasn't very good in bed, but he was polite."

Julianne knew from previous mind reading encounters with prostitutes that as much as young men believed in their sexual prowess, to a seasoned professional, most of them resembled fumbling idiots. She didn't want to stand out, so she kept the false memory consistent with what Polly would expect.

"He talked briefly of leaving town. You do not expect to see him again."

CHAPTER TWENTY-THREE

Marcus shuffled his boots on the coir mat outside the inn. It was the third one he had tried—the last one he had visited was full, and the first was closed, apparently for health violations if the notice nailed to the door was accurate.

He ducked his head through the low doorway and hailed the man at the bar. Already, it was teeming with people.

"Any rooms?" Marcus asked over the din.

The innkeeper shrugged. "Sorry. We had to take in the people from Bitch Alley."

That was the name of the inn that had closed. "Anywhere else I can try?" Marcus asked.

The man shook his head. "Look, if you're desperate, you can sleep in the bar. We don't close until midnight, though. Used to be later, but the curfew put a stop to that."

"Curfew? Has there been trouble in town?" Marcus asked. In Arcadia, that would be the only reason for restricting the movement of citizens.

The innkeeper shook his head. "Those new pricks in town think it's *unseemly,* or some shit. Got in old George's ear and convinced him to make it law. Damned lucky the lord loves his booze, or they'd have shut us down completely."

Shaking his head, the man turned away. He stepped over to serve a burly man in crisp linen when a woman shrieked.

"You bastard, Emmory!" Heels slammed against boards as a furious woman stomped downstairs and into the bar. "I can't believe you went and fucked that little trollop!"

A weedy man carefully stuck his head out, then ducked as the girl picked up a nearby mug and pegged it at his head. "Adeline, it was just one night!" he protested.

"You said we were getting *married*! Instead, you gave me *crabs*, you asshole! You… you slimy little cunt fucker."

Marcus bit down on the inside of his cheek. For some reason, the foul language spewing from the pretty girl's mouth seemed hilarious.

She turned a scathing gaze past him. Slamming a key down on the bar, she snapped at the innkeeper. "I'm going home. You saw me pay for the room—well keep the money. Just don't let that limp-dicked, lice-infested little creep back in. It's MY room, and he's NOT allowed in it."

The innkeeper grinned. "My pleasure, love. Mind if I give it to another patron?" He nodded at Marcus, who cringed at the attention.

The girl regarded him a moment, then nodded. Then, she leaned close. "Here's a tip. Don't sleep with the village whore the night you elope with your girlfriend, or she'll cut off your balls."

Marcus coughed, wondering if it was possible to feel any more uncomfortable than he did now. "Ok?"

She smiled a brilliant grin. "You can have the room. Might be best to burn the sheets, though. Never know what you'll pick up in a town like this."

Turning, she flounced out the door. "I'll send a man for my things!" she called behind her.

The innkeeper just shook his head. "Crazy, bloody women,"

he muttered. He shot a glance at the man—Emmory, Marcus guessed—and flicked his thumb towards the bar. "You heard the lady. I'll bring your shit down, but you're not stepping foot back in that room."

Emmory nodded, then slunk over to a booth and slid down into the seat looking miserable. For a moment, Marcus felt sorry for the man. The feeling quickly vanished when a serving girl walked up to offer him a drink, and Emmory immediately started flirting.

"Doesn't look like that marriage was ever destined to last," he commented.

"He didn't know a good wicket when he was on it," the innkeeper said. "Name's Jones, by the way. I'll send one of the girls up to clean the room. And, er, change the sheets."

Marcus laughed. "That'd be appreciated. How much do I owe you?"

Jones lifted his hands and shrugged. "You heard the lady. It's already paid for."

"Thanks!" Marcus stood. "I'll go get my things."

He went out to the crowded stable and unlaced the packs tied to the two horses. Carrying his things in, he caught sight of the furious maiden across the street. Her face was streaked with tears and when she saw him, another fat drop rolled down her cheek.

"Do you have a way to get home?" he asked, concerned.

"Y-yes." Adeline hiccuped. "My footman is looking for a carriage to hire. Surely, someone will have one when they find out what a desperate situation I'm in?"

Feeling awkward, Marcus nodded. He wondered if he should stay until the young woman had company when she suggested he do just that. "Anyone could see me here, weak and vulnerable. I wouldn't want some brute to take advantage of that." She caught his sleeve and tugged it gently, looking up with big, bright eyes.

"Err... sure." He hitched one of the bags over his shoulder, using it as an excuse to move slightly away.

Adeline moved closer. "You know, I really didn't love Emmory. I was just so desperate to get away from Father. He's such a beast—always keeping me home, when I could be visiting the city, meeting eligible husbands. Why, my cousin Dora had the most wonderful party the other week, and he made me leave at midnight! Things were just getting exciting."

Lifting an eyebrow, Marcus didn't comment. He didn't think she would appreciate him siding with her father.

"And bringing me to a place like this to get married! I thought he was taking me out of the city, to a far-off estate near the sea. He had no taste, none at all. Just think what my life would have been like!" One hand lifted to her brow and she swooned, stumbling into Marcus. He jumped back like he'd been burned.

"Oh," she giggled. "I'm dreadfully sorry."

"No, that's ok. Um… you're sure your footman is coming, aren't you?" He craned his neck to look down the street.

"Unless…" her eye widened. "Unless he's abandoned me! Oh, sir, please would you take pity on me if he has? I can't return home alone! There are bandits, and thieves, and Bitch knows what else out there."

"I'm sure he'll come," Marcus said, desperately hoping it was true. He stepped back again when she lunged at him.

"Wait, I know! I could stay with you! Where are you from, one of the neighboring estates?"

A carriage pulled up on the street nearby and Marcus shot a glance at it, hoping it was the footman.

"I… came from Tahn," Marcus explained. He didn't go into detail about where he had come from before that—he didn't have a chance.

Adeline stepped back, eyeing him up and down. "You come from a farming village? And you dare speak to me? Young man, do you even know who I am?"

"I'm pretty sure you spoke first," Marcus said. He straightened, able to look her in the eye now that she wasn't drooling on him.

"Nonetheless, you have no right to bother me. I am Lady Adeline, daughter of Lord George the Second. I am far too important to be spoken to by a commoner like yourself."

Adeline picked up her skirts and flounced across the cobbled road, narrowly missing a rider coming through at a trot. She stumbled, glared at Marcus as he reached out to help, then stormed off to the waiting carriage.

"Bitch take me, both his kids are assholes," Marcus muttered to himself.

A short man flung a door open, then had it snatched out of his hand as Adeline slammed it shut. The footman jumped onto the seat behind the horses and they flopped off down the road, sending up a cloud of dust that tickled Marcus's nose, making him sneeze.

"Bless you."

He spun to see Julianne approaching from behind.

"Did you find us a place to stay? I hope so—it's almost sundown and I'm starving." She rubbed her stomach for emphasis.

"Oh, thank God. I was almost attacked." Marcus grabbed her arm and led her into the inn.

"Attacked?" Julianne asked, shocked.

"Yes. A woman jumped me, and I'm pretty sure it was with the intent of marrying me—that is, until she got the idea I was a lowly farmer. That made her back off pretty quickly."

Bewildered, Julianne just shook her head.

"Is she gone?" Emmory stuck his head out of the door.

Marcus groaned. "Yes. Now leave me the hell out of it."

"What, she try to hit on you?" Emmory snorted. "I knew she didn't give a rat's ass about me. Oh, well, I've found a softer pillow to cuddle tonight."

A hand slapped the side of his head, and he ducked back in.

Marcus resolutely kept his eyes averted as they entered the inn and walked past Emmory's table. Still, Marcus could have sworn there was more than one woman eating dinner with him.

"Let's get a meal sent up to the room, shall we?" he said to Julianne.

"Oh, I'd *much* rather eat down here," she said. "Because there just has to be a story behind what just happened, and I'd much rather hear it in front of him." She jabbed a thumb at Emmory's table.

"I hate you," Marcus muttered.

Julianne laughed as she leaned over the bar. "Can we have two meals brought up, please? I don't care what, as long as it tastes good. A bottle of wine, too, if you have something old and red."

"Got some aged sweet wine, it's going on about five years now." The bartender pointed at a customer loading up flatbread with some kind of spicy bean mix. "That's the special. It's got some kick to it."

Julianne nodded eagerly. "It smells amazing!"

She headed upstairs after the innkeeper told them which room was theirs. "One of the girls are in there, stripping the sheets," he said. "She'll be done soon."

In fact, she was just on her way out of the room with an armload of linen. "All done," she said with a grin. "Though I think I need a shower after touching these." With a mock shudder, she skipped downstairs.

"There's so much more to this story than I know," Julianne said, collapsing on the double bed.

"What, you didn't just read the mind of the dozen people that saw it unfold?" Marcus asked.

"I'd rather hear it from you." When Marcus gave her a skeptical look, she explained. "Have you ever heard a story told that was so funny, the person telling it couldn't speak? Or seen something just plain stupid, only to have the stories told about it turn out better than the event?"

Thinking about it, Marcus realized it was true. Sometimes, it wasn't the story itself that was funny, it was how it was told, or who was telling it.

"I don't get to do that. Not often, anyway. In the Temple, everyone knows everything almost before it's happened. So, go on, tell me!"

Humoring her need for a good story, Marcus told her what happened between the lovers, and outside the inn with Adeline. Seeing how much Julianne enjoyed the story, he played up the details and acted the part of the young seductress with gusto.

When someone knocked on the door to drop off their meals, Julianne was rolling on the bed, hysterical. "Oh, my.. And *you...*" She screeched again, holding her stomach as she laughed.

"Oh, no," she gasped. "I can't eat like this!"

Her eyes shone white as she forced herself into a deep meditation, then flickered back as she giggled again.

Eventually, the hunger overwhelmed her mirth and she dove into her meal. "Oh, Bitch's flames, that's *hot!*" Fresh tears, this time from the spicy lentils, slid down her cheeks. Still, she emptied the plate, gulping down wine to cool her tongue.

"Careful with that," Marcus warned. "It's not mystic's elixir."

"Oh, I can handle my wine," Julianne said. "Had plenty of practice with the guard."

Still, she shook her head when Marcus offered to top off the glass. Her muscles were soft and her skin warm and tingling. "What a day. It's barely sundown, and I'm ready for bed."

"You sleep," Marcus said. He hopped off the bed and pulled down a corner of the freshly laid blanket. Then, he spread his bedroll on the floor beside it.

"Oh, don't be an idiot," Julianne admonished. "Sleep next to me. I swear, I don't have lice."

That made them both dissolve into laughter again. Marcus carefully stacked up the plates and glasses, and left them outside the door by the now-empty wine bottle. "If you're sure," he said.

He stripped down to his underwear and slid into bed. The maid had left a bed warmer between the sheets, and he groaned as his feet found the warm spot. "That feels divine," he said.

He rolled over to nestle in beside Julianne. He rubbed her arm, sending goosebumps down her flesh. Nuzzling close, he pressed his nose into her hair. She smelled of jasmine and wine, and he smiled happily.

"Can you tell what I'm thinking now?" he whispered in her ear.

His only response was a light snore. Ruefully laughing at his string of bad luck, he snuggled in and closed his eyes. In a few minutes, he was asleep.

CHAPTER TWENTY-FOUR

Bette eyeballed the man in front of her. Jake was far taller than her, and yet the short woman still seemed to tower over him.

"Now, either get yer ass back in that line, or fight me like a man who has an actual pair of balls." Bette slid a glance to Sherp, a gangly youth in the second row. "No offense, Sherp." Sherp reddened, swallowed and nodded.

He had lost one of his balls after a drunken run through what he thought was an empty field. Even fueled by rum and terror, he couldn't outrun the angry bull he had disturbed.

"Now, what's it gonna be ye big lump of shite?"

Jake's eyes dropped to the ground. "If it's alright with you, Sargeant, I'll take my place in line."

He shuffled back and Bette resisted the urge to kick him in the balls anyway. From the sidelines, Garrett gave her an approving nod. She scowled back. *Don't need yer bloody approval, ye bastard,* she thought, uncaring that he couldn't hear it.

"Now, do it again ye soft cocks! Try ta do it at least as half as well as the only real soldier in yer bloody troop." Pointing at Sharne, who already held her spear overhead perfectly straight, Bette grinned.

"Yes, *SIR!*" Sharne yelled a bare second before the others.

Bette ran them through drills three more times, cursing out the slow and the slouched, those with poor form and worse balance. "Ye think ye'll stop an army with that limp dick?" she asked one young man before jabbing him in the forearm.

The spear clattered to the ground, and he picked it up, chagrined. "Sorry, Sir."

When she finally let them go, they were tired and sweaty. Even Sharne's form had begun to suffer, a telltale wobble in her spear tip showing her fatigue.

"Off with ye, then," Bette yelled. "Go feed yerselves some breakfast and do some real work."

The group of villagers slumped in relief.

"Hey now, don't cry, ye pussies. That was the best bitch-damned training we've had! I never seen progress like this. Better than a guard troop of pubescent rearick, ye are! We'll have ye trained ta fight dragons with toothbrushes in another week or two!"

Some of the men grinned at that. She had spent the last session telling them how fast that pubescent group of rearick would kick their asses.

"Do ye think they'll survive in a real fight?" Garrett asked when they had gone.

"Aye. Marcus has been training them well. They've got the forms, they just need the strength."

"And if they're tired and aching when the attack comes?" Garrett picked up the spears left behind by the trainee fighters and started stacking them in the makeshift rack.

"Then we teach them to fight tired and aching." A hard glint to Bette's gaze made Garrett want to know more, but afraid to ask.

She saw his curious look. "When I finally convinced Henrick to teach me fight skills, he told me the day I began was the day I'd get trounced the moment I left. The cadets I learned with weren't exactly known for forward thinking. I got beaten every day for three weeks. I didn't have the luxury of resting, and I'm bloody well stronger for it."

Garrett knew she'd had a hard time. She was the first female fighter in... well, ever. She had fought tooth and nail to be accepted by the rearick as a fighter, and for the most part, she had won. It hadn't come easily, though.

"I trust ye know what yer doing. Do ye want to check the rosters before I post them?"

"Eh, I trust ye know what yer doing." As she echoed his words back, she winked at him.

He coughed and looked away. Ever since they had fought at the festival, Garrett had treated her as his superior. By their traditions, she was. He had no idea how to feel about his superior flirting with him, though.

"Annie should have breakfast laid out by now." He left the unspoken question hanging in the air.

Ruefully, Bette shook her head. "Clumsy shits broke two more spears. I'm gonna fix those, then get another half-dozen made up. I know they're the easiest weapon to learn, but Bitch knows I wish Marcus had taught them swords."

"And where would those swords come from, then?" he reminded her.

"Aye, true. Still, even shovels might last longer. They might even do some damage."

Garrett laughed and waved goodbye. "Send a runner if ye need me. I'm off ta feed me face, then I'll check on the guard stations."

"Give them hell if ye see them sleepin' on the job!" she called after him.

"That I will, lass," he muttered to himself. "That I will."

CHAPTER TWENTY-FIVE

Bastian collapsed at the small patio table outside the makeshift classroom. He pulled out the fresh roll Annie had sent him off with. She knew he had an early first class, and didn't want him to miss breakfast.

"Thank you, Annie," he muttered through a mouthful of food. "That woman is a blessing from the Bitch herself."

"Bastian! Just the man I wanted to see." Danil strode up, clapping Bastian on the shoulder. Behind him trailed Rhea, one of the young women from the village.

Only in her early twenties, Rhea was the closest to Bastian's age. They had chatted at Mary's a few times, but he didn't really know her. She stood out amongst the townspeople—quieter than most, she was also one of the smartest. Bastian had seen Julianne beside her, both girls bent over a book or scroll, Rhea's dark skin offsetting Julianne's paleness.

"What can I help you with?" Bastian tried to settle a sudden feeling of foreboding. When Danil smiled that widely, chances were, it meant trouble for everyone around him.

"I have a new project for you."

"Project?" Bastian asked. "I have my next class in a half hour, then I need to see to Francis."

"It's Francis that got you into this. Rhea here," Danil gestured to the girl, who blushed. "Needs some magic training."

Bastian frowned. What the hell is he up to? "I have room in my next session, but these students have already mastered basic shielding. We're working on strength now." He took a long swallow of water from his skein to wash down the suddenly dry lump of bread.

"Oh, Bastian." Danil grinned and laid a hand on Bastian's shoulder. "I don't mean mental magic. Young Rhea has the makings of a druid!"

Bastian choked, spitting out the water. He dabbed the wet dribble down his shirt. "What the fu—uhh. Sorry, Rhea"

Rhea giggled. "Don't worry, Master Bastian. I've heard worse words outta my pa's mouth."

Ignoring her protest, Bastian turned back to Danil. "Seriously, what are you thinking? I don't know the first thing about Druidry. And did you listen at all when I told you about the disaster with Francis?"

"See, Rhea, I told you he'd do it. But if you guys only have a half hour, I'd better leave you to it." Danil waved at Bastian, whose face glowed an angry red.

"You can't just—" Bastian threw the rest of his bread roll at Danil's retreating back. "*YOU OWE ME!*" he yelled.

"Anytime!" came Danil's fading voice.

Bastian's shoulders dropped in defeat and he heaved a long sigh.

"Geez, I'm not *that* bad, am I?" Rhea plonked herself down in the chair opposite Bastian. "Look, I think this is crazy. I don't have magic—I failed out of Danil's shield class, and I think he feels bad. I'm not like Lilly. I just… you know, like my pets."

As if in response to her words, a tiny mouse peeked out from her collar. "Squeak," it said.

"Can you talk to it? Make it follow instructions?" Bastian asked wearily.

Rhea laughed. "I trained Molly with cheese, that's all. It wasn't magic."

Feeling a flicker of hope, Bastian asked, "How many other pets do you have? How many are trained?"

"Seven mice, four dogs, two cats, nine birds and a roach," She beamed proudly and Bastian's heart fell. "Oh. Right. That's not really normal, is it?" Rhea looked crestfallen for a moment, then brightened as she realized the implications. "Wow. If I really have magic… Wow!"

Bastian allowed his head to drop into his hands for a moment. Then, he harnessed his mystic professionalism. "Don't get too excited. You could just be good at what you do."

"So… you don't think I have magic?"

"Everyone has magic. Some people just can't seem to tap into it like others. Here, talk to your mouse or whatever it is you do." Bastian tucked his water away and rolled up the empty cloth that had held his lunch.

Rhea slowed her breath, held up the mouse and started whispering to it. As she did, her eyes shimmered with green, like Bastian's did when he used magic, but weaker and a different color.

"Ahh, dammit." He threw the wadded cloth at the ground. "Looks like I've got another student."

Startled, Rhea almost dropped the mouse. It squeaked loudly as she dropped it in her sleeve, then clapped. "Bastian, that's so exciting! What do I have to do?"

She waited patiently while Bastian racked his brain for anything he knew about nature magicians. Though Rhea was not and would never be a true druid—she would have to train with the forest people to earn that title—her magic was like theirs.

"Look, I don't think I know enough to really get you started. Have you ever spoken to Lilly? She could run rings around what I know about animal magic."

Rhea shook her head. "I've asked her help before, when one of my pets got sick. She was happy enough to assist, and fixed little Myra up no trouble, but she refused to breathe a word about her abilities." Rhea shrugged, embarrassed. "I won't lie. I've always been a little jealous of her magic."

Bastian sighed. "Very well. Let's start with the basics."

He told Rhea to stand quietly, concentrating on her breath. "Now, reach inside. Feel the connection with your animals."

"Squeak!" Milly poked her head out again.

"Did I do that?" Rhea asked.

Bastian had no idea. "Why don't we try another animal. One you're not close to." He looked around and spotted a lark in a nearby tree. "What about that one? See if you can make it come here."

"Ok." Rhea shook out her hands, stretched her neck, then dropped into a relaxed posture.

Bastian watched as she stared at the bird, brows furrowed into a small frown of concentration. Her breath slowed. Green sparks shimmered in her eyes.

Bastian's heart jumped when the bird cocked its head and flew closer, landing on the garden fence. It chirped, then let out a cry before jumping to the ground.

Rhea opened her eyes and gasped. "Oh… I did do that!"

A second bird fluttered into the small yard, then a third. A crow swooped at Bastian's head, and he yelped.

"Rhea? I think we should—" His words were cut off by the screech of more birds, swooping and diving and circling overhead. He yanked Rhea's arm, dragging her into the schoolhouse.

"What the hell was that?" she whimpered. "I take it back. Magic sucks."

Bastian pulled back a curtain, jumping back when a nasty looking bird flapped over to it and tapped at the glass with its beak. One eye peered into the room and the bird let out a low 'caw'. Beyond it, the yard was teeming with birds. They flapped and waddled, covering the yard and tripping over each other as they meandered past the open window.

"I don't think we should go out there," Bastian said in a low voice.

The bird by the window tapped again, this time harder. The crack jarred Bastian's nerves, and he let the curtain drop. "This is actually freaking me out more than when Francis tried to set me on fire," he muttered.

"Did you say something?" Rhea was peeking through a crack in the wall panelling. She jumped back when a sharp 'rat-tat-tat' sounds from the other side of the wall. She rubbed her arms. "Bastian… what if they don't go away?"

A solid knock on the front door started Bastian's heart thumping all over again. "Who—" he cleared his throat and tried again. "Who's there?"

"Oh, for crying out loud." Lilly shoved the door open and strode straight to the back of the small building. Her hair frizzed out angrily and her face was stern. "What are you *doing* to those poor creatures?"

Bastian eyed her warily, wondering how such a small child could look so intimidating.

She flung the back door wide and carefully stepped out, making sure she didn't disturb any of the birds. "I'm *so* sorry, little ones. They didn't mean any harm, and they won't do it again. Go on… fly away."

One, then two birds flapped their wings and took off, followed by two more. Then, in a mess of caws and loud flapping, they rose like a writhing blanket and took off into the sky.

Lilly stormed back in. "Really, Bastian, for a grown up you don't have a lot of sense. I'd expected more from you."

Too stunned by the tiny girl's wrath to respond, Bastian just stared. By the time he found his tongue, Lilly had stomped away, slamming the door behind her muttering something that sounded like "stupid boys".

"Well," Bastian said, sitting down with a thump. "I guess that means your first lesson is done."

CHAPTER TWENTY-SIX

Julianne smoothed the fabric of her wrinkled dress against the bedspread. "Marcus, this looks awful! I can't turn up to a theatrical performance like this." She flopped back on the bed. "I'll just have to fake it."

"Or," Marcus said as he whipped the dress away from her. "You can do what normal people do at an inn, and ask for what you need." He walked out, the door swinging shut behind him.

Julianne rolled herself off the bed and pulled out her bag. She had packed expecting to take audience with a lord, so at least she had enough to make herself presentable. When Marcus returned, she was perched on the edge of the bed with a small mirror in one hand, and a powder-dipped brush in the other.

"Oh. Uh, sorry." He blushed, averting his eyes.

"Marcus, I'm not naked. It's just a shift." She rolled her eyes as swept the brush along her cheekbones.

"You're in your underclothes!"

"You wouldn't even know that if I threw on a belt and did my hair."

She had a point. The linen shift was edged with lace and came down past her calves. It certainly didn't show enough flesh to warrant beetroot cheeks and a sudden stammer.

"Besides," she added. "I've stood next to you in the middle of a brothel full of bare assed women. I know you've seen worse."

"Yeah, but they weren't—" He stopped, swallowed, and turned away. He hung the dress on a hook before kicking through a pile of clothes to find his scabbard.

"Oh, good," Julianne remarked. "A sword will be less conspicuous than magitech."

"Who says I'm not taking both?" he asked, strapping the leather belt around his waist then sliding a gleaming sword into its home. "We have no idea what we're up against. I'm not taking any chances."

Julianne touched the powder to her lips and smudged it. Checking her face in the little mirror, she smiled. "That'll have to do. I miss Zoe—that girl could work a masterpiece with a little powder and gloss."

Marcus passed the dress to her. "You don't need Zoe. You look stunning."

It was Julianne's turn to blush. "Thank you, Marcus." The dress slid over her head with a quiet swish, and she yanked the laces tight. Throwing a gold belt around her waist to finish the outfit, she let her eyes mist over as she reached out to connect with her surroundings.

The meditation allowed her to focus inward, and she realized her shoulders were tight and her stomach bubbling with nerves.

Don't be a fool, she admonished herself. *There's nothing these charlatans can throw at you that you can't handle.*

"Are you ready?" Marcus asked.

She nodded, then kissed his cheek when he swept the door open for her.

The innkeeper had given them directions to the theatre tent, but Julianne soon realized she shouldn't have bothered asking.

People meandered along the street in the falling light, all headed north towards a warm glow that reflected off the low-slung clouds.

A little way up the street the road turned, revealing a giant billowing tent, made of daffodil silk that rippled in the stiff breeze that raced through Muir. It plucked at hats and flapped at coats, flinging leaves across their path and whipping Julianne's carefully combed hair into her face.

Julianne grinned as a shiver ran down her back. The bright lanterns drew her closer to the tent as the noise of excited chatter swelled.

"I don't think I've ever been to the theatre," Marcus remarked. His eyes were dark against the twilight backdrop and sparkled with joy.

"Just make sure you remember why we're here," she reminded him.

Together they climbed the small hill that led to the small pavilion at the tent's entry. A woman with fine whiskers protruding from her nose and furry, pointed ears greeted them. She turned to show her tightly-clad silhouette and purred at Marcus.

"Two tickets, please," Julianne told the attendant.

The cat woman leaned forwards, her generous chest tightly bound in the clinging costume, and licked her lips at Marcus.

"Refreshments are in the small tent on the side there. You're early, but it fills up quick, so get yourself a good seat, love!" A fluffy striped tail rose as she waved them away, attached to her wrist by a fine string.

Julianne jabbed Marcus in the ribs. "Stop ogling. You look like you've never seen a woman before."

"Oh, I've seen women," he said, voice hoarse. "Just not women like… that."

Raising her eyes to the stars beginning to dot the sky, Julianne shook her head. "Can't take you anywhere, can I? First the brothel, now this!"

"Hey, I met you in a brothel," he protested.

"I'd been working with you for weeks before that!" Julianne tugged his arm and led him through the wide tent-flaps.

"You were Stellan, then," he pointed out.

Julianne spotted a section of seating down in the front that had been lined with thick cushions, and a table set up nearby held a bottle of wine and a plate of cheeses.

Julianne pointed it out to Marcus. "That's where our George will be."

"Yes. The perfect spot for his bodyguards to keep an eye on him." Marcus motioned to the doors that overlooked the seats, then showed her a small door directly across that led to the area behind the large stage. "That's probably for the performers, but I bet it's no coincidence that the lord's seat is so close to it."

They went to sit nearby, taking the row behind the padded seats. Being a level higher meant Julianne would be able to look over George's shoulder and, with any luck, speak to him.

The arena quickly filled, and Julianne and Marcus were soon sandwiched between well-dressed people chattering about the upcoming show.

"Did you hear they've added a water display?" the woman beside Julianne asked her. "My neighbor's daughter saw them practicing, hanging about from wires and swimming like fish. How clever! I simply don't see how they could outdo the last variation, though."

"I've never been," Julianne told her. "Are they really that good?"

"Oh, yes, dear. So good that Lord George himself is their patron. That's why they don't travel anymore, he simply insists they stay. Very good for the economy, you know. Oh, here he comes now! I *do* hope he sits nearby."

Julianne turned to where she pointed. Sure enough, a resplendently dressed man strode into the tent. Milling spectators quickly moved out of his way, encouraged by two stern-faced guardsmen that waved shiny cudgels at anyone slow to jump.

"Interesting choice of weapon for a bodyguard," Marcus murmured.

Julianne frowned. She quickly dipped into the minds of the guards, who were occupied with keeping an eye out for anyone who might mean their liege harm. Both of them carried a feeling of unsettled wariness that they couldn't quite finger.

Julianne guessed it was the beginning of a mind trick, meant to make them quick to anger and retaliate against citizens who put a foot wrong. That would make the populace afraid of the guards, and more compliant... well, in theory.

Arcadia had shown that people crushed by an unfair rule *would* revolt. She would have to keep an eye on those two.

When she brushed against George's mind, she was surprised to find it solidly blocked. Instead of pushing against it, she drew back, thinking.

The woman packed in next to Julianne gasped as the lights dimmed. "They're starting. I can't wait!" She gave an excited little clap, then settled back to watch the show.

"Ladies and gentleman, take your seats and sit back. You're about to embark on the journey of a lifetime!" The whispering voice hissed through the room, quelling the last of the conversation.

A rustling sound made Julianne turn. Behind her, slowly coming down an aisle between the long bench seats, a dark-hooded figure approached the front of the tent. Julianne's heart lurched, but as the figure came closer, she saw the costume lacked the signature gold trim and insignia of the New Dawn's robes.

Instead, this person wore heavy black robes that obscured the face. The only clue to the person beneath was a slender hand peeking from a sleeve to hold up a canister of smoking incense.

Julianne inhaled, the scent of smoky musk and jasmine hitting the back of her throat and warming her nostrils. She sat back, waiting until the display began before making any move to approach her target.

Bright lights flickered on to shine down on the stage from an intricate contraption that used mirrors and lanterns to focus the light. The spotlight drew back so that the mechanical arm was hidden by a swathe of silk.

"Welcome to an adventure like none you have seen before. I am Enigma—I shall be your guide."

A woman stood in the middle of the stage, skin glittering in the light.

"Is that costume painted on?" Marcus whimpered.

Julianne looked a little closer. "You know, I think it might be."

Whatever the performer was wearing, it clung to her skin, shimmering as she moved. She spun, twirling like a dancer as a gong boomed. The movement made her taut muscles ripple.

"Watch out, you'll drool on your shirt," Julianne said with a smirk.

Marcus snapped his mouth shut with a click, then gave her an embarrassed grin. "She's not as pretty as you."

"The hell she's not," Julianne retorted softly.

There was no denying the performer, with her soft, dark hair and too-big eyes was a beauty. Even her breasts didn't—

There's no way that's possible, Julianne realized. The performer continued to dance, contorting her body. Her long hair swung delicately, but flicked in the wrong direction during a complex movement. She reached out to Marcus.

They're using an illusion, she sent.

Before the thought was complete, she realized that his shields were entirely down.

She had to pull herself back before she slipped right into his mind—he had often dared her to read his mind, but with his natural ability to shield, it was always a conscious effort and even then, most of his thoughts were tucked into neat little compartments behind their own, secondary shields.

She had never touched on those, worried about invading his clear need for privacy. Seeing him laid bare like this was a temptation, even to her.

Jabbing him in the ribs, she touched her temple. He jumped, frowned, then squinted. Brushing his mind, she saw his defenses were still down.

Something's wrong. The thought blared out from his mind, and Julianne placed a hand on his leg to stop him jumping to his feet. He looked down at it, and Julianne was unable to block out his rather loud mental dialogue.

I can't shield. Why the fuck can't I shield? His eyes widened. *That means she's reading my mind! She heard that. I know you heard that, Julianne.*

It's ok, Julianne sent. *I won't take advantage of you. Not unless you ask me,* she added with a wink.

"Our story begins on an island that never was, a tiny speck floating across the sea. Long have adventurers and seafarers sought this magical land... for here, and here alone, can the Fruit of Apollo be found."

The light swung, picking out a willowy tree that swayed in an imaginary breeze. Bright orange fruit, glowing with a vibrancy that made them seem to emit light, dangled from branches in heavy clumps. Enigma floated over, steps so smooth that she looked like a ghost drifting across the thick grass beneath her feet.

She reached out a hand and plucked a tiny fruit. "Such fruit has never been tasted by mortals. This is the fruit of gods." She tossed it into the air and it flashed, disappearing as flavor exploded in Julianne's mouth.

Oh hell, she realized. *Marcus isn't the only one unshielded.*

Kicking herself for not checking earlier, Julianne created a mental shield. The effort took more out of her than she expected, and she touched a hand to her forehead. It came away damp.

Carefully, Julianne created a light illusion to disguise her eyes, then sent out a mind-reading probe. *Well, at least my other abilities don't seem to be affected.*

As the gasps and awe of the crowd touched her senses, Julianne brought her attention back to the stage.

Enigma had finished her dance. A cloud of fireflies twisted across the stage before flying into the air. They froze, twinkling like stars.

"...and as the sea rose, the island was swallowed by the water."

At Enigma's cue, water pooled on the ground. It bubbled and rose, touching first the shoes of the patrons, then rising to soak pants and dresses. The audience shrieked with excitement and joy as it quickly filled the tent.

The ladies' silks floated and hair drifted in the gentle current, but the water was warm and whatever illusion was at work stifled any fear in the tent. The water was far above Julianne's head before she realized she was still breathing normally.

A quick glance at Marcus confirmed he did, too. Though bubbles clung to his skin and his hair swayed as he turned his head, his voice was normal when he spoke.

"That's one hell of a trick, Jules. You don't think it's one of them, do you?" he whispered.

The thought had crossed Julianne's mind, but she shook her head. "I can't see how the New Dawn would benefit from this, except financially. If it's a coincidence, though, it's a hell of a big one."

Everyone in the makeshift theatre was mesmerized by the performance. At a call from above, all eyes turned upwards just as three acrobats swung down on fine wires, spinning and drifting over the stage like waterborne mermaids.

Julianne murmured a quiet word. Once she was sure nobody was paying attention to her, she stood and made her way to the little door by the stage. No one reacted. With one last backwards glance, she slipped through and closed it behind her.

CHAPTER TWENTY-SEVEN

The tiny ale house was quiet. The lanterns had been dimmed, and Mary glared at Danil and Bette from her side of the bar, pointedly wiping down the bar in between large yawns.

"So, ye'll speak ta Bastian on her behalf?" Bette asked.

Danil nodded. "Sure. Bastian's got plenty of experience training up the different magical skills."

He didn't mention the string of accidents that had resulted from it, afraid it might scare Sharne away from developing what seemed to be a talent for some kind of physical magic.

"You're not sure it is magic yet, though, are you?" he asked carefully.

Bette shook her head. "I still think she's just fast, but Garrett swears her eyes changed when she smacked him down. Of course, he might just be soothing his poor broken ego."

Danil laughed. "After what you did to him, I'm surprised he has any ego left."

"Aye," Bette chuckled. "I did give the lad a thumpin'. Had ta do it, though, the little prick was acting a right twat."

"He hasn't given you any trouble since?" Danil asked, swirling the last of the ale in his mug. He tipped it up and gestured to Mary for another.

Mary sighed as she filled it. "Look, you two obviously aren't going anywhere. I've had a shit of a day, though, and I need to be up early to squeeze a class in before I open up." She tossed a jumble of keys on the table. "Turn the lanterns off when you go and lock the door. Drinks are on the house, but don't go crazy. And don't leave a mess."

She stretched, and reached back to rub her back before untying her apron and dropping it on a nearby table. "See you in the morning, Danil."

"Thanks, Mary," he called back.

Danil had organized the early morning classes himself, noting that many of the working residents struggled to fit them in around their daily duties. Between those and the night classes, which Bastian would be finishing up about now, they had covered most of the village.

"Garrett's a good man," Bette said, continuing their previous conversation. "Not bad on the eye, either."

Danil raised an eyebrow, but didn't answer, taking a long swig of ale instead.

"In fact," Bette said, picking at a bit of crusted food on the tablecloth, "I was thinking I might ask him ta step out with me."

Drops splattered the table in front of Danil as he choked on his drink. "You what, now?"

"Step out. Ye know, ask him fer a date." Bette shrugged, her face ruddier than usual. "Unless ye think he'd say no?"

"It's been less than forty-eight hours since you punched him in the face. You don't think you should wait a bit?"

"Aye." Her eyes dropped and she looked away.

Danil brushed her mind and immediately realized he'd made a mistake. She thought he was dissuading her because he'd seen something in Garrett's mind to show he wasn't interested. "No! I mean, I was only guessing. I don't know what he thinks, I have no idea. Really!"

Perking up a bit, Bette straightened. "Ye think I have a chance, mystic? Because that man is a right specimen, he is." She sighed wistfully. "That is, when he's not being a giant prick."

Danil winced. "Bette, this isn't exactly my area of expertise. Last time I got involved, I damn near got myself killed." The memory of Julianne's icy gaze made him shiver. "Just… do what *you* think is right."

"Eh. You're as useful as tits on a bull. What's the bloody use of all yer mind-readin' oobey goobey if ye can't help a lass out?"

"I promised him I wouldn't read his thoughts, Bette." Right now, Danil thanked his lucky stars he had. He didn't want to get any deeper into this mess than he was.

"Fine." Bette's chair scraped the floor as she pushed it back. "Finish yer drink while I go wash the pitcher fer Mary, then I'll walk yer blind ass home."

Danil grinned as he waved his empty cup at her. "I'll help you clean up, then I'll walk your short ass home, aye?"

"I'd have a better chance of making it on me own than you," Bette said.

Danil snorted. "I'll have you know I've memorized every step in this village."

"Not drunk, I'll bet." To prove her point, Bette spun around and shut her eyes.

A moment later, a clatter and a curse made her spin back. "Fine," Danil grunted. "Not drunk."

Chuckling to herself, Bette cleared the table.

CHAPTER TWENTY-EIGHT

Julianne sucked in a breath of clean air, glad to be away from the cloying incense. The tiny backstage room was crowded with costumes that were piled onto hangers and stuffed onto shelves.

A small corner table almost sagged under the weight of paints, powder tins, and brushes. Above it, a large mirror reflected the lantern light and gave the room a cozy feel.

Julianne quietly walked over to a curtain that cordoned off the far side of the room. She nudged it slightly to one side with a finger, then stepped past it.

This room was bigger. Clean sawdust covered the floor and a more orderly assortment of dresses, headpieces, and cloth strips lined one wall.

"I'm sorry, this area is for performers." The voice made Julianne jump. She hadn't seen the old lady in the corner, dressed in black with a lace veil over her eyes. "Let me show you back to your seat."

"I came—" Julianne's attempted lie faltered as someone slammed into her mind. It was a blunt attack, and she fought it off, slamming back against her shield to strengthen it. "Who are you?" she growled.

"I am Madam Seher." She rose a hand in a quick gesture. "And you, my dear, are in trouble."

Hands grabbed Julianne's arms. She struggled, kicking out with a foot and trying to twist away. She failed.

A cloth was pushed against her face and she coughed, snorting in acrid fumes before she could think to hold her breath.

Her shield dissolved as fatigue swamped her bones.

Her mental attacker forced past the remnants of Julianne's defenses, knocking aside her feeble attempt to summon her magic.

"What did you do to me?" Julianne mumbled, her mouth too numb to speak clearly.

Madam Seher didn't speak. Instead, she lifted her veil to reveal glowing white eyes.

The presence in Julianne's mind twisted and Julianne fell to her knees even as she coldly evaluated her opponent.

She was strong, but Julianne was stronger… or, she would be if she could summon a scrap of magic.

Julianne's shields were down, and they weren't coming back no matter how hard she tried. Her muscles were limp, too weak to even lift her head, so fighting wasn't an option.

Seher pushed further into Julianne's mind, picking out memories and examining them one by one then discarding them to move onto another.

"Let her go." The cloth dropped away and Julianne sucked in clean air.

The strong hands let her down gently. Madam Seher took the cloth off the brawny man and stood over Julianne.

"I apologize for that. Times aren't safe, and we had to be sure."

"Sure of what?" Julianne asked. She coughed to clear the thickness in her throat and pushed up with her hands. She lifted her head, looking towards the curtain as it flew open.

"Found another, Mai—Madam Seher." The man who'd attacked Julianne held up his prize.

Marcus stood carefully still to avoid pricking himself, at least until he saw Julianne on the floor. He lunged forwards in the big man's grip and kicked backwards, a strike that should have snapped the man's knee and brought him to the ground.

"Be still." Seher's white eyes blinked as Marcus slowed to a stop. "Jakob, make sure you don't let him go this time? Not until we've explained."

"Explained what? Who are you?" Julianne asked.

Madam Seher smiled. "Why, we are the resistance, my dear."

Julianne shook her head. "What are you resisting?"

"The same thing you are. That man, Rogan. He and his lapdogs turned up in Muir not long before we were due to pass through on a tour. By then... well."

"Bastards have old George wrapped around his finger. The young bastard, too, not that he needs incentive to be a cunt." Jakob grunted, his face showing the distaste he felt for the young lord.

"There are a dozen or more of Rogan's mages installed in the palace," Madam Seher continued. "I don't know who—some wear the blue, others seem to have integrated into the household and the guard. We've done what we can to protect Lord George, but I fear we have reached our limits. We move out in a week."

"We can help," Julianne said. She stood, brushing off her dress and hastily erecting a mental shield. "We ousted them from Tahn, and came here to take Rogan down for good."

"You came here afraid for the people you rescued. You don't have the numbers in either place to fight the Dawn." Sadness touched Seher's features. "As much as I wish you did."

"You don't need an army to take down one man," Marcus pointed out.

"You do when that man *is* an army. He and his generals are too strong. You won't be fighting them, but all of the innocents they control." Seher folded her hands. "And I won't stand by while the innocents of Muir are slaughtered in your quest for vengeance."

"It's not vengeance," Marcus protested.

"Yes, it is," Julianne said quietly. "They killed my people. They infested my Temple. I will have vengeance, but Madam Seher is right. The Dawners in Tahn deserved what they got. None of them needed persuading to hurt those people, the mind control was to keep them from rising against Rogan and August."

"How do you know this lot are innocent?" Marcus asked.

Julianne shrugged. "We don't. That's the problem. He's come to a city, surrounded himself with people that can—that *will*—get hurt if this turns into a war."

"What?" Marcus blustered. "We just go home? If we do that, how many innocents will get slaughtered when George's shit-head son comes to pillage our own?"

Julianne shook her head. "I didn't say we're going home. We just need to be careful, that's all. We're in a stronger position now we have allies, and—"

"We won't be joining you," Seher said sharply. "It's too danger-ous. I won't risk my people, and I won't start a war."

Julianne's eyes narrowed. The older woman had a hard, unflinching gaze, but something didn't add up. "Who are you protecting, then?" she asked. "You introduced yourself as the resistance. A resistance doesn't lay down and let the bad guys run them over. What's your plan?"

The corners of Seher's mouth turned up. "Clever girl. You won't get an answer from me, though."

"You can have one from me." A hidden door in the back wall swung open and a young woman stepped out.

"Adeline?" Marcus gasped.

"You know her?" Julianne asked.

He blushed. "No. Nope. Absolutely not."

Adeline laughed. "Apologies, soldier. I didn't mean to drag you into my ruse." She stuck a hand out to Julianne, who shook it despite her confusion. "My name is Adeline. Lord George is my father."

Marcus groaned. "That fight with your boyfriend in the inn?" he asked.

"Not my boyfriend," she laughed. "One of Seher's men. I had to pass on some sensitive information. The Dawn don't like the theatre group, they know most of the troupe have magic of some kind. They haven't been brave enough to take them on, but they might if they realize they're involved in conspiracy and treason."

"Lady A, please don't use that word," Jakob begged. "I'll do what needs doing, but I'd rather not think about it, you know?"

She chuckled and reached up to put a hand on his shoulder. "We're liberating the people, and our rightful leader from an insidious force. Is that better?"

Jakob nodded with a wide smile. "Much."

"Adeline, you know it's too risky to be seen here," Seher chided.

The girl shrugged. "It's risky for me everywhere. Besides, August keeps leering at me, and it's making my skin crawl."

"Punch him in the balls," Jakob grunted, a flash of anger for a brief moment.

"You know I can't draw attention to myself like that. They'll lock me up in a heartbeat, they only ignore me now because they think I'm a flighty, useless moron." Adeline looked to Madam Seher. "Adding more people to our cause can only help. What do they have?"

Seher sighed. "A handful of mind-mages. This one"—she gestured to Julianne—"is terribly strong, the others less so. They have a bunch of villagers barely recovered from the Dawn's attack, and a couple of… what were they called? Roricks?"

"Rearick," Julianne confirmed. "Two of them, both furious fighters."

"Furious drinkers, by what I saw in your head."

"That, too," Julianne laughed. "But they really can fight.

Marcus is even better than that, and he has a natural gift for shielding, at least when he's not snorting anti-magic smoke."

"Wait. You mean they drugged me? With incense? I knew it! There's no way someone got through *my* shield without some kind of sneaky trick." He settled back with a smirk now that his honor had been restored.

"It's the only way to make our performances effective," Madam Seher admitted. "We'd have hidden it from the Dawn, but we'd already put on three shows before we found out what was happening. We didn't want to change anything, in case it drew more attention to us."

"What was your plan before we came along?" Marcus asked.

Seher shrugged, turning a shoulder away from him. "Protect our lady. Everything else has hit a dead end. We can't find Rogan; we don't even know what he looks like. We just know he's here, somewhere. George has ordered him away, and imprisoned, and beheaded, but he just returns once the guards have 'forgotten' their leige's instructions."

"So, why haven't they taken the city? And how is George resisting?" Marcus shot questions at her like quick barbs.

"George is like your man here, blessed by the goddess with an iron mind. As for the city? I'm guessing they don't have the strength," Seher explained.

Julianne thought for a moment. "They can't control a whole city, probably not even an army. Once they move out of range, most compulsions wear off and mind tricks dissipate. If the people care for their lord, they'd revolt at any outward moves by Rogan to take control."

"Right," Adeline said. "Though, their numbers have grown since August returned a few weeks ago. Whatever he was doing in Tahn, I think he's trying to replicate it here, on a larger scale."

"We need to take them down," Julianne said. "The methods they use don't rely on mind tricks. They torture and brainwash, even kill. If you don't cut the rot out now, it'll infest too deeply to remove it without destroying lives."

Madam Seher's eyes fell. "I've spent my life keeping my family safe. All those performers… every one of them was beaten or shunned for their gifts. I helped them to see the beauty in themselves, and kept them safe. I can't risk them. Not without a better plan."

Julianne's heart ached. "I know. I won't ask you to."

"But—" Marcus spluttered.

Julianne shook her head. "I was happy to fight for Arcadia and for Tahn. I wouldn't ask others to die for either of them, though. You can't make someone fight. It has to be their choice."

"Thank you," Madam Seher said. "I will help if I can."

"So will I," Adeline said. "But I agree with Madam Seher. We need a plan. A good one."

Julianne pursed her lips. "I might have one, if you can get us a private audience with your father."

A smile spread across Adeline's face. "Tomorrow night. I'll send a carriage for you."

"Tomorrow, then," Julianne said. She nudged Marcus. "If anyone asks, you're going to see your secret lover."

"And where will you be?" Marcus spluttered.

"Right beside you. No one will see me, though."

"Bitch's britches," he muttered. "What am I in for now?"

CHAPTER TWENTY-NINE

The heels of Julianne's boots clicked on the cobblestones as they headed home through quiet streets. They had stayed with Madam Seher and Adeline until well after the show had finished, fine tuning their plan.

Adeline would let slip to her father she had created a scandal —*another* scandal. Rogan had little interest in her love life and would likely leave him be for their discussion. Adeline would steal George away, and Julianne would stay back to impersonate him until she could take down the New Dawn.

"You're sure this is a good idea?" Marcus asked.

"If you ask me that again, I'll brainwash your mouth shut for the rest of the walk," Julianne joked.

"So, you're not the least bit worried about kidnapping the local lord?" he pressed.

She shrugged. "We're not kidnapping him. Ade said he's pretty agreeable when his lapdogs aren't close by. He knows what they are, and he'd do anything to get rid of them."

"All it'll take is one Dawner to get in his head and for him to cry out for help. We'll have the whole city guard on us in a heartbeat."

"Once we have him, I can keep him safe," Julianne reminded him.

"And who's going to keep *you* safe?" Marcus asked.

"You are, of course. George isn't the only one going missing, and I can easily disguise the two of us for a while."

"You have way too much faith in a simple city soldier," he said. Still, her confidence in his ability made him stand a little straighter… at least, until he realized what she'd meant. "Bitch's honor. You're going to turn me into Adeline?"

Julianne grinned. "You've got the legs for it," she pointed out. Then, she stopped walking and caught his arm. "Marcus, I have faith in you. You're one of the best fighters I've seen, and I'd trust you with my life."

"Only one of the best?" he asked, eyes wide with shock. "Julianne, I'm hurt!"

She slapped his arm and he winced. "Smartass." She took off again, not waiting to see if he was still beside her. "Last time I give you a compliment."

"Oh, no, don't stop. It's good for a man's constitution."

"Bitch's sake, Marcus, I'll never tell you you're good at it again!" Julianne rolled her eyes, but grinned at him, her white teeth flashing in the darkness. They rounded a corner and the warm lights from the inn brightened the night.

"That's not all I'm good at." At her glare, he raised his hands defensively. "Fine, fine. Look, I'm going to do a little recon before our adventure tomorrow." Marcus said.

"Now? It's the middle of the night!"

Marcus shrugged. "Best time for it."

He checked to make sure his weapon was strapped to him and that his pocket was full of coins. He might need them if he got into any difficulty. He might not have mind control, but he did speak a universal language: Money.

"I'll be back by dawn. Don't get into any trouble while I'm

gone." He winked, then stepped back into the shadows. A moment later, he was gone.

With a groan of frustration, Julianne pushed open the door of the inn. Without a second glance at the bartender or the few straggling drinkers still seated at the tables, she dragged her tired body upstairs. She had slept poorly the night before, not used to the thin, lumpy mattress.

"It's going to take one hell of a meditation to work these knots out." Julianne rolled her shoulders back and stretched her neck as she slipped into her room. Dropping her robe on the floor, too tired to do anything more—she sprawled on the bed.

Someone jumped on her. Hands pressed her arms and legs into the bed and a painful blow slammed her skull. Lights flashed, then dimmed as she lost consciousness. A moment later, she was bundled into a sack and tossed out the window into a waiting cart.

CHAPTER THIRTY

Annie thumped the heavy pot of porridge down on the table. "All I'm saying is, I expected her to have sent a message by now."

"Julianne is more than competent," Danil reassured her. "I'm sure she's fine."

Annie's mouth twisted. "Mark my words, you'd best have those pointy sticks at the ready."

Danil sighed, but when Francis gulped down his food and left in a rush, a heavy lump of unease settled in his gut.

After breakfast, he went to find Garrett. "How go the troops?" he asked.

Garrett rubbed his beard. "Well enough. They can point a spear without stickin' it in their asses well enough. Can't say I'm happy, though."

"What's wrong?" Danil asked.

"Just seems like we're running out of time. Julianne and Marcus have been gone a few days now. Surely they'd have sent word?" Garrett finished lacing up his boots. "Either way, I plan ta ride them hard and get 'em as ready as I can. Might pay to increase the watch, though."

"I'm surrounded by worry warts," Danil muttered. "I suppose a few more on guard can't hurt. Can you fix the schedule?"

Garrett nodded. "Aye. The reality be sinking in now, they know that if young Julianne doesn't talk us outta this, we'll have a real fight on our hands. It's one thing stabbin' a stick at a sack of straw, quite a bit different to shovin' it through a man's belly."

"Or having it stab back," Danil pointed out.

"Aye. Ye think ye could spare some time today? I'd like ta put our top recruits through one of those conjured up battles ye do."

Danil agreed and they set a time. Just as he turned to go, Garrett cleared his throat.

"Oh, err… before ye go, there's something I wanted to talk to ye about."

Danil winced. "What's that?" He could guess the answer and would have given a sack of gold to avoid the discussion Garrett was so eager to have.

"Well, it's about Bette. Ye see, I canna get her outta me head."

"Try harder?"

Danil's advice fell on deaf ears. "She's unlike most I've ever seen, lad! The way she swings that wee axe of hers, and the look in 'er eye when the battle madness hits her…" Garrett grunted in satisfaction, his eyes glassed over as he imagined his rearick princess flying into battle.

"Bitch's balls, Garrett. Just ask her!"

"Are ye crazy? She might swing that axe at me head. Or worse, she might say no! Do ye have any idea what kind of hurt that does to a man?"

Heaving a sigh, Danil wondered just how deep he was getting. "Garrett. She likes you. Just ask her out before I die of old age. Please?"

Garrett chewed on a stray whisker. "Ach, yer right. I should just do it."

"That's the ticket! Now, I'm going to go hunt down Francis and see how his wall is going."

"Aye. Yer worried too, aren't ye?"

"Aye." As much as he didn't want to admit it, Danil was.

He didn't expect to hear from Julianne, not until she had secured a solution to their problem. But this was the third day now, and George Junior's deadline was growing closer every minute.

"Chin up, lad." Garrett slapped his shoulder. "Yer lass is a clever one. She'll be fine, and she'll save the day. Not the first time, won't be the last."

"I have no doubt about that," Danil grumbled. Julianne seemed to attract trouble. World-ending trouble, sometimes.

CHAPTER THIRTY-ONE

A cold, hard surface pressed against Julianne's face, chilling her skin. She lay still, eyes closed as she listened.

Someone breathed nearby, a quick, hard sound. They were stressed. But was it because they were about to hurt her, or because they had been caught in the trap with her?

Grit pressing into her flesh suggested she was on a dirty floor, but wasn't grainy enough to be outside. No light seeped in between her eyelids, so it was dark. Carefully, in case she was being watched, she cracked an eye open.

A small barred window above her let streaks of flickering light in to bounce off the heavy stone walls. Wincing as she turned her head, she noted she was in a tiny room—more of a cell, really—and someone was leaning against the wall beside her.

"Marcus?" she whispered.

He jumped and bent down to examine her. "Are you ok? Thank the Bastard, Jules!" He helped her to sit up and held her steady as her stomach turned from the movement.

"Where are we?" she asked.

"In the bowels of the lord's manor. It's a proper dungeon

down here." He kept his voice low, suggesting someone was close enough to hear them.

Julianne narrowed her eyes, trying to force past the throb in her head to summon magic. Marcus shook his head. "The guy that slammed the door on us said we're being guarded by Dawners. No tricks, or he'll send one in to thump us."

"You believe him?" Julianne whispered.

He shrugged. "Probably best not to test his theory until you're ready to go full mind-fuck on them."

She gave a soft snort at his description of her powers.

"I'm serious, Jules. When you're up to it, no half measures. You get in their heads, and you fuck them up. We can't risk calling any more people down here than you can handle."

Julianne nodded, then winced as it made her head pound harder.

Marcus noticed. "How's your head?"

"Nothing broken. It'll hurt for a few days, I'll bet."

She stopped talking when footsteps clomped down the hallway. The metal doorway clicked and a small hatch opened at the bottom. Someone slid a plate of food through, then a water flask before it slammed shut. It clicked again. *There's a lock on the outside,* Julianne realized.

Marcus watched her as the boots stomped away. He didn't ask if she had managed to harness her magic—her clear eyes suggested she hadn't. Without letting his disappointment show, Marcus passed her the water.

"Drink. It'll make you feel better."

She took a small sip of water, rolling it around her mouth. Then, she took a long swallow. "That does feel a bit better," she said.

Picking up a roll of bread, Marcus let his eyes drift towards the small grate in the door. He had spent an hour calling out for help when they had first locked him in here. When Julianne's comatose body was tossed in later, he'd stopped. Clearly, there would be no fair trial and no audience with the city lord.

A bite of the bread made him screw up his face. *When I get out of here*, he thought, *I'm going to kill whoever decided to feed us cold stew and stale bread.* He let the roll drop back to the plate, then offered Julianne some.

She nibbled at the bread, dampening his fear about her head injury. It's the first place he would attack a mystic—addle their brains and reduce their spellcasting, it was just common sense— but he wouldn't forgive whoever had caused that injury.

"You've blood on your face," he said. Marcus dampened a corner of his shirt with water, and used it to clean Julianne's face.

"How long have we been in here?" she asked, her face close enough to tickle his eyebrow with her breath.

"You missed breakfast." He finished and moved back. "You're lucky. The cooks here couldn't hold a candle to Annie. Hell, even Danil can make better food than this lot."

Julianne shuddered and Marcus could imagine what she was thinking. The one time they had let Danil cook, they had all decided to go hungry rather than eat the mucousy slop that landed in their bowls, or the bread rolls that *thunked* on the table like stones.

"So, lunch time, at least," she murmured.

"Maybe. It's too dark in here to really judge, but I'd swear that was dinner they just fed us, not lunch." He rubbed his stomach, wondering if maybe he was hungry enough to risk that congealed stew after all.

"I suppose a few herbs for an aching head is too much to ask." She slumped back against the wall. "Marcus, what the bloody hell are we going to do?"

"Nothing we *can* do," he replied, settling back next to her as comfortably as he could. Against cold, knobby stone that wasn't very comfortable at all, but he was used to roughing it.

"Bullshit." She gave him a halfhearted slap. "We can plan. Tell me exactly what happened."

Marcus had been accosted in the street outside the inn. He had scouted the town, chatted to some lowlifes who had told him which of the guards could be bribed. Of course, that information itself had cost him a few coins.

He hadn't found out much more than they already knew—the local soldiers had escalated from being generally well-respected peace-keepers to roughneck dictators, using violence to control the citizens of Muir. Of course, most of that behavior was directed at the lower end of town.

That the nobles hadn't yet been targeted rankled Marcus. Back in Arcadia, he had seen what could happen when the class divide had stretched too far. Lord George had, so far, ruled Muir fairly. Marcus's quick jaunt through the slums showed them to be in pretty fair condition.

They were clean, for slums, and not as crowded as he had expected. Fresh water pumps were plentiful in the streets and, though closed so late at night, more than one market stall was erected in the area, showing that the locals had access to trade.

Satisfied with the information he had collected, Marcus decided to head back to a warm pillow to try and catch an hour or two's sleep before morning. He had just rounded the final corner when some thugs jumped him, slipping a sack over his head and tossing him in a carriage.

They had left him bagged and bound for the journey, only untying him after he was safe in the prison cell. They hadn't spoken much, but Marcus had easily recognized the blue robes of the New Dawn on two of the five.

"Five? They sent five men to take you down?" Julianne didn't sound entirely skeptical, but Marcus saw one of her eyebrows climb a little higher than usual.

He puffed out his chest. "They must have heard the rumors."

"Which one?" she asked casually. "Was it the story of how you dissolve into a quivering mess every time a sex worker strolls past? Or the one about the lady who almost had your pants around your ankles before you shook her off outside the inn?"

He glared, and she couldn't contain her laughter any longer.

"The rumors about my superb fighting skills, smartass," he said. "You know, for someone with so much responsibility, you don't act like it sometimes."

Julianne's giggles softened into a sigh. She leaned against him. "I'm just lucky enough to have friends who remind me what life is really about."

"What's that?" he asked.

"Fun. Everyone deserves to have fun and to laugh. Even the poor and the downtrodden. That's why I fight for them, Marcus. Because they deserve to laugh, too."

"These bloody Dawners don't agree," Marcus reminded her.

"And that's why I'll wipe them from the face of the planet." Though her words were harsh, she spoke softly, snuggling into him. The knock to the head and the long night had caught up with her. Minutes later, she was asleep against him.

CHAPTER THIRTY-TWO

By the next morning, Danil's nerves had begun to set in. It had been too long, he was certain Julianne would have sent a message by now. He loaded some bread with fried onions and dumped it on his plate, then poured some water.

"Garrett, what's the chance of putting a few scouts on the outer perimeters? If that army comes knocking, I want as much notice as possible."

The rearick looked up, pulled from his deep thoughts. At least, Danil thought he had been thinking. He might have just been scowling for fun. Never can tell with a rearick, he admitted.

"Easily done, Danil," Garrett said. "There were a couple of guard trainees that dinna quite make the cut. Brave enough, and quick enough, but not quite smart enough to figure out which end of the spear had the point, if ye know what I mean." Garrett stroked his beard, thinking.

"Don't send fools. We want them to send back messages, not get killed." Danil shoved another bite of ham steak in his mouth and chewed it quickly. "And I want extra men on those walls. It won't take long for those bastards to breach them if we aren't protecting them."

"Aye, I sorted that last night. Bette suggested we move training ta the front gates. Means if something happens, our main forces will all be there together."

Danil nodded appreciatively. "Good idea. Francis back in training yet?"

"Nah, he's obsessed with these bloody defenses. The man treats Julianne's word like an instruction from the Queen Bitch herself." Garrett eyed the last hunk of bread in the middle of the table.

Danil nodded towards it. "You can have that, I gotta run. And don't talk shit about Francis. You know if Julianne said jump, you'd be on the roof in a hot second."

Garrett laughed. "Aye, it wasn't an insult. Francis is doing a damn good job on that wall. I can't believe how fast the lad's done it!"

"He had help," Danil reminded him.

"Aye." Garrett fell silent again and Danil couldn't help himself.

"You're thinking so hard you're at risk of an injury, rearick. What is it?" Danil swallowed and stood, waiting impatiently.

Garrett ignored him.

"Fine, you hairy little prick. Go fry your brain while I slave away in the classroom."

"Go fuck yerself," Garrett responded good-naturedly. "When yer done, can ye send young Bastian down ta have a natter?"

"Will do." Danil grabbed his hat and his long walking cane. He took it everywhere now. The villagers and his friends were all so busy, he was often caught walking about town on his own with no one nearby to mind-read to see where he was going.

"Don't walk into any walls, ye hear?" Garrett called out as the door swung shut behind Danil.

"Yeah, yeah," he muttered. "It was only that one time."

The walk to town was a slow one, and the sun didn't quite manage to warm him before he got there. He threw open the classroom door and gave a dramatic shiver. "Brr! It's colder than a witch's tit out there." Bastian, Rhea, and Lilly all looked up

"Forget your coat?" Bastian asked mildly. "Sorry, Lilly. Go on."

Danil shrugged an apology to the young girl and gestured for her to continue whatever she had been doing when he barreled in.

"So, if they start getting cranky at you, just think of the nest and let the magic go, or they'll come and peck your eyes out." Lilly's own eyes glowed green with a mischievous sparkle as she said this and a moment later, Rhea almost fell off her seat when a raven tapped briskly on the back window.

"Lilly," Bastian said sternly.

She had the grace to look at least a little ashamed. "Sorry, Bastian. Sorry, Rhea."

"It's ok, Lilly," Rhea said when she had regained her composure. "Thank you for taking the time to teach me."

"Are we finished?" Lilly asked, looking at Bastian enquiringly.

"Next batch of eager students will be here shortly," Danil confirmed.

"You may go now, Lilly. And thank you!" Bastian called after her as she darted out the door. He shook his head in wonder. "The way she runs out like that, you'd think she didn't want to be here."

"Are you even sure she does?" Rhea asked.

Bastian smiled gently. "Positive. She enjoys showing off her skills, and she really does want you to learn, Rhea. She just isn't used to this kind of structure."

"She's also a kid and thoroughly enjoying having one over on the grown-ups," Danil added. "She might be a little odd, but she's still a pretty typical nine-year-old in a lot of ways."

"And now I'm odd, just like her," Rhea said with a frown. She caught Danil's disapproving look.

"Oh, I didn't mean it like that. Lilly is delightful, and everyone in town loves her. It's different though, you know? She's a child, she's supposed to be vague and flighty, so having magic doesn't seem like a big deal."

"And that's precisely why magic is so bloody hard to come by in this region!" Danil griped. "It's an esteemed profession, or it should be. People should feel encouraged to embrace their gifts, not shunned for it."

Irritably, he shuffled Bastian's papers off the tiny desk and shoved them in the drawer while pulling out his own. He set them down with a thump before continuing his tirade.

"Do you really think the New Dawn would have had such an easy time of it if this town was full of fire-throwers and mystics? Or if you'd all learned to shield as children, or had an army of wild animals fighting on your side?"

He slammed his hand down on a table in frustration, then looked up to see Rhea's startled face. "I'm sorry," he said quietly. "I just wish we'd sent people here earlier. To teach you and to start changing some of the attitudes that exist in small towns like this. Maybe then you'd have it a bit easier."

It was Danil's turn to feel startled as Rhea slid her arms around him, pulling him into a hug. "Thank you," she said.

"What for?" he asked. Before he had time to find out, she was gone.

"Women," Danil muttered as Bastian stood.

"Nice speech. Does that mean you're staying when all this is over?" Bastian had shared his grand idea with Danil already—a magic school, one for all talents unlike the segregated teaching centers back in Arcadia. He wanted to create a place where children and adults could come and explore the possibilities magic offered, and learn to accept and rejoice in their gifts.

"Perhaps." Daniel's roving mind picked up two men approaching. "Hey, my students are here. Garrett wanted to talk to you, though."

"What about?" Bastian asked hesitantly.

"Not a clue."

"Still holding fast to that promise not to read his mind?" Bastian asked. "If he wants to ask me for relationship advice, I'm running for the hills."

Danil laughed. "I hope it is. I don't want to be the only person knee-deep in rearick love."

Rolling his eyes, Bastian grabbed his robe. "I'll be back after lunch. Try not to set anymore hearts on fire, aye?"

CHAPTER THIRTY-THREE

August finally slipped the narrow peephole in the cell door open. Both prisoners shot to their feet, looking far too energetic after two days in a dungeon with only the worst slops to eat.

He had listened to them complain about the food, almost caught himself laughing at their description of it smelling like 'moldy goat dick', then banter with each other about how one would know what that smelled like.

Now, August pressed against their shields, letting a small smile touch his lips as both of them scrambled to reinforce their mental defenses. His own shield was impenetrable, reinforced by looping his magic through two other magicians.

He let the mystic girl batter his own shield for a moment, then opened the cell, gesturing for two of his bodyguards to enter first. They, too, were cordoned off from any attacks, protected by another trio of mind-linked magicians.

The entire party was safe from this girl, despite the overinflated rumors of her strength.

August stepped over to the boy and chuckled at his defiant growl. "You think you can defend against me?" he asked.

Slamming into the soldier's shield, August was surprised at the resistance he faced. Distracted by the effort, he didn't notice the girl move closer. In a flash, her fist whipped out.

August jumped back and his guards grabbed her, but not before the boy crumpled to the floor. The foolish girl had just knocked out her companion. "Come now, I'd think the leader of that so-called Temple would realize a little knock to the head won't stop me?"

"Oh? Try getting in his head," she said with a smirk. Her eyes were bright white, showing she was using some kind of magic other than a simple shield.

Cautiously, August did. Instead of a solid shield, he waded into a murky sludge that coated the young soldier's mind. He recognized it immediately. It was a spell that pulled the victim into a coma, usually used for surgeries or to ease the suffering of a painful death. He wouldn't be using the boy's mind now, not as long as she stayed connected to him.

Unworried, August shrugged. As long as her attention was there, she wouldn't be using her magic for anything else. "A soldier will stay with him. Your magic won't protect him from a slit throat. However, if you co-operate, neither of you will be harmed."

Julianne nodded with all the composure August expected from someone in her position. He walked off, leaving his soldiers to drag her behind him.

When he pushed open the doors to the formal chambers, he did so with a grin. His dear Master, Rogan, would be so proud of his work. August had sent the men to capture Marcus and Julianne, and had been the one to find them and bring them here.

These thorns in his master's side would now be pawns in his game. "Master, I bring you a gift!" The joy that filled August when he saw Rogan smiled was unequalled. "This is the girl that Donna failed to bring to you."

"You think she'd be here if not for me?" the red-haired witch spat.

August sneered at her. "I think that if I'd gone to the Heights, Tahn would still be ours."

"And who was in control of Tahn when it was lost?" she asked sweetly.

"*SHUT UP!* Your squalling bores me." Rogan lounged in the oversized, wooden chair, one leg hanging over the arm. He ran his eyes over Julianne appraisingly. "Girl, do you know who I am?"

Julianne nodded calmly. "You're the ass maggot who lost Tahn."

Rogan sat up straighter, his ice-blue eyes flashing. He didn't slip into a trance, though. Instead he laughed. "Finally, someone who has a backbone."

"What, sick of your fawning little minions and all the other people you have to mind-fuck so they'd like you?" she asked.

August took a step towards her, hand already clenched in a fist meant for her pretty little face. Rogan raised his hand, and all desire to punch the woman vanished. The thought that August may have displeased his master twisted his gut and made him want to cry.

"Why didn't you accept my invitation?" Rogan asked, his eyes piercing Julianne.

"Because I'm not a power-hungry psychopath," She retorted. "Why did you invite me? Couldn't you find anyone who'd play with you willingly?"

Rogan laughed again, slapping his knee. "I like this girl!" He sobered, expression dropping to a blank canvass as his eyes faded to white. The connection between August and Rogan meant the slave could sense his master's unstable emotions and feel the magic he used.

August breathed deep as Rogan pressed against Julianne's

shields, looking for a chink. Though the girl still had her soldier boyfriend bound in a coma—he had left a trio of mental magicians to ensure the guard that left with him remained safe—she managed to hold up a good front.

"Really, though. Why would you pass up the chance to rule the world? Didn't you believe I could do it?"

Julianne's face hardened. "What I didn't believe is that anyone could be such an arrogant dick. Much less a mystic. You literally have the power to walk in people's shoes, to feel their emotions and experience their pain. How can you be so ignorant?"

Rogan held up a hand to examine his fingernails. One was trimmed crooked and August felt Rogan's irritation prick at him through their bond. Picking at the offending nail, Rogan sighed.

"Truth be told, I was never that good at the whole mind-reading thing. Compulsion? Sure. It was the only way I could get my father to feed me as a child." His eyes flicked up at Julianne, still white.

"So, you used your pathetic skill to cover up your failings." Julianne's face was flat, and anger fanned in August's chest.

How dare she speak to the master like that? He readied himself to attack her. Surely, Rogan wouldn't stand for her insolence.

"You have no sympathy for a neglected child? I thought people like you were all about the injured and the weak." Rogan pushed harder against Julianne's shield.

"I believe anyone should have the freedom to make mistakes, as long as those mistakes don't affect the freedom of others. You hurt people, Rogan. You used them and spat them out. Others, you killed."

"You're talking about your mystics? Ah. Yes, that was unfortunate. Also, against my orders." His eyes cleared a moment as he looked around. "Donna? Come here."

Donna almost tripped over herself as she raced over to the master. She knelt, breath coming in quick gasps.

"Master? You said I was forgiven for that. Please don't be mad." She clasped her hands together, trembling at his feet.

"You have displeased my guest, and that displeases me." He leaned closer, gabbing Donna's face and tipping it up so she looked at him. "*You* displease me."

Donna's chest heaved as she sobbed, clawing at Rogan's robes and begging him to forgive her.

"Should I kill her?" Rogan looked to Julianne. "Or would you like me to torture her a little first?"

"Please, Master, I'm sorry. I'm so sorry. Please don't send me away." Snot streamed down her face unchecked.

Julianne turned her head away from the pitiful sight. "You're a sick bastard. You're going down."

She lunged forward and Rogan jumped up, embracing his magic again. A guard grabbed for Julianne and missed. She darted forwards, but was intercepted by another soldier.

August threw himself at Julianne barely a moment after Donna knocked into her. All three tumbled to the floor as August clawed at the mystic's face. Seeing a clump of hair, he grabbed at it, coming away empty handed.

"What the…" He scrambled back, eyes darting from side to side. "It's a trick." He ran to Rogan, who stood watching in the middle of the room. "It's a trick!"

Julianne—a second Julianne—appeared in the doorway to the council chamber. Then, another. This one slipped inside and locked it behind her, then pulled out a slender dagger.

"Illusions!" August screamed. He lunged for the one with the weapon, and it vanished.

Rogan felt a spike of fear that shot August through the gut. He dove for his master. "Get down!" They tumbled to the floor, but Rogan rolled away.

"Shut up, fool," he snapped, eyes white.

Pounding on the door, accompanied by yelling, signaled the

guard had arrived. Rogan had drawn them here with his magic and August cursed for not thinking of that himself.

With a shaking, creaking crack, the door burst open and the chamber filled. Soldiers ran forwards, armed with steel and teeth bared in a magic-induced rage.

CHAPTER THIRTY-FOUR

Marcus looked down, glad to see he was back in his own clothes. The illusion Julianne had put on him back in the prison cell, swapping their appearances so she could take control of his mind, had worn off.

He couldn't believe they had pulled it off. Once August led Marcus out of the room, he had been sure the gig would be up. Julianne was a true Master, though—she had held onto the illusions, convincing August that he was her, and the cell guard that she was an unconscious Marcus.

That left Julianne free to work on the guard and the mystics downstairs, while Rogan watched Marcus pretend to cast magic. Marcus's shields had kept Rogan out of his head, and he had been none the wiser… that is, until all hell broke loose.

Now, Rogan and August had vanished, and they were facing off with a dozen guards.

Marcus slammed his fist onto one man's face, then pivoted to kick another in the kneecap.

"Jules, we gotta run!"

"Not until we take down Rogan," she snapped back, eyes white as her—well, one of the illusions of her—rolled between two guards and sprinted for the door. That Julianne vanished as another twirled in front of him, stabbing at a guard with a rusted short sword.

The guard dodged, stumbling back into another Julianne who stabbed him in the neck with a knife. Blood spurted from the wound and Marcus looked at her in relief.

"Phew. I was starting to wonder which one is you."

"Did you see which way he went?"

Marcus shook his head. "He vanished, the thin air sort of vanish."

"Shit." She kicked at a guard, then buckled as another jumped on top of her. Marcus started as she dissolved into nothing.

"Take your eyes off that girl for one second..." he muttered. Then, louder, "We have to retreat."

"Ok," another Julianne said beside him, this one clean and bright eyed.

"That's not at all weird," he gasped as a boot struck him in the back.

"Run, now!" two Juliannes snapped. He bolted for the door, almost tripping over an illusion of himself just ahead. Another was on his heels, flanked by two of Julianne.

Together they plunged through the door, chased by guards, and fled. Each pair went a different way, Marcus taking the left passage with another of himself, before a hand yanked him around a corner.

Julianne grinned, panting, and pressed a finger to her lips. A false Marcus sprinted past, followed by two guards that didn't see the real him standing against the wall.

"This way," she whispered, dragging him by the arm to a nearby doorway.

She hustled him through, then down a side passage and up a narrow staircase. "That window leads to a courtyard. If we can get down, then scale the wall, we're home free." Her eyes still glowed white, and he guessed she wasn't just hiding them, but scanning the minds of anyone nearby for a map of the building.

She stepped out onto the window ledge and he followed. "Jules, I feel like a sitting duck up here," he murmured. "You sure no one will notice us?"

She nodded, face pale. The strain of her magic was showing, and that was a really bad sign.

Marcus quickly scouted the courtyard. "Slide over that way," he said, gesturing along the narrow ledge towards a large tree. "We can jump to one of the branches."

"And I suppose I'll just hide the movement of an entire tree, just like that?" she asked with a raised eyebrow.

Still, she moved towards it, one hand feeling along the white-washed stone for support, the other gripping his tightly. Her skin was cool and dry, he had to give her credit for that. Anyone else —him included—would be sweating up a storm.

"Steady does it," he said as she approached the nearest outstretched branch. The willow swayed in the breeze, the thick branches looking suddenly frail over the hard ground below. "Find your center. Don't jump until you're balanced."

"Marcus, I'm a mystic. I do nothing *but* find my center." She quickly grinned, dropped his hand and threw herself into the tree, letting out a low "*Oof!*" As she connected with a branch.

She hung for a minute, legs dangling as she clutched the shaking limb, then pulled herself up, kicking at her skirts to find purchase on the bark. Once she was settled, Marcus leaped across, landing in a crouch on a broad branch.

"Smartass," Julianne said. "Just had to show me up, didn't you?"

"Hey, I'm not the one casting a half-dozen spells while balancing in a tree." He reached out to take her hand and help her down a branch. She yanked him back, almost overbalancing him, then put a finger to her lips.

"...get away? Are they all stupid, or just the ones loyal to my father?" Boots stomped beneath them as George the Third stormed through the courtyard. "It doesn't matter. My men are ready to march. We'll wipe their shitty little town off the map once and for all. Then, we'll come back and take care of that bitch-damned circus full of traitors."

"I'd advise against it, my lord." Marcus stifled a growl at the sound of August's slithering voice. "They have quite a number of magicians."

"Who, the town or the actors?" George snapped.

"Both, my lord." August allowed a note of condescension creep into his words, but George either didn't notice, or didn't care.

"That's why you're coming with me. Bring ten men, you can catch up with us on the road. Hell, bring twenty if you think we'll need them. They can't be allowed to…"

The voices faded and Marcus didn't catch August's reply. It didn't matter. "We have to go," he whispered.

Julianne nodded. "We have to warn Madam Seher first."

He waited for her gesture to proceed, then slithered down the wide trunk onto the ground and darted over to the wall. He gave Julianne a boost up. Once she had caught the lip, he jumped and heaved himself over.

"That looked like an effort," Julianne sweetly pointed out. "Getting soft, are we?"

He rolled his eyes. "Just tell me when to go," he said.

CHAPTER THIRTY-FIVE

Madam Seher listened to their hurried explanation, her expression darkening by the minute.

"If they're onto us, they know about Adeline. We must get her out. Did you see Lord George at the manor?"

Julianne shook her head. "Not in person, and not in any of the minds I could skim. A couple of maids wondered where he was, and his bed wasn't slept in last night."

Seher cursed. "We must go back. That man and his daughter are vital to this city."

"You're crazy," Marcus said. "You need to get your people out while you can. We need to return to ours."

He turned to go, but Julianne caught his arm. "She's right. George and Adeline are... they're not like anyone you've seen before."

He gave her a flat faced stare. "I've meet Adeline, remember?"

Julianne shook her head. "Not like that, Marcus. Madam Seher showed me. She and George are kind and just, their citizens adore them. If they fall, the town will be ripe for the picking by anyone, and very few people would step in for the good of the people."

"You go," Madam Seher said. "You need to get back to your people. Mine can take care of Adeline and George."

"Bring them to Tahn when the fighting is over," Julianne said quickly. "We'll keep them safe until we can remove Rogan from the city."

Seher nodded. "Queen's favor to you."

It was an old saying, usually reserved for those who held Queen Bethany Anne, also known as Queen Bitch, in high standing. Though the term 'bitch' had come to mean something less respectful now, it was once a term of honor to the woman who first brought magic to the world.

"And to you," Julianne replied.

Clasping hands, the two women said a quick goodbye.

"Do you think they'll make it to Tahn?" Marcus asked as they hurried away.

"No idea," Julianne said, her eyes already white again as she pulled him back behind a corner. A moment later, two men strode past.

Julianne took Marcus's arm. "We are two upper-class citizens out shopping," she whispered. "Don't look scared, and don't look for trouble. I'll tell you if we need to duck."

Marcus pasted a smile on his face and nodded happily at the next person they passed. Without making it obvious, he took a quick look at his clothes. Julianne had dressed him in illusionary silks and fine leather boots. She was robed in soft purple linen, embroidered with tiny, white flowers.

"You look like you need to take a shit," Julianne murmured.

"Don't all rich people?" he asked.

She laughed, the sound attracting the attention of a soldier. Julianne's hand tightened reassuringly on Marcus's arm, so instead of bristling, he stared the man in the eye and mouthed "women!" As they passed. The soldier chuckled, and went about his business.

As they approached the gate, they slowed. "Bit of a crowd there," Marcus pointed out. "Can you sneak us past?"

Julianne drew them back into a shadow. "I think so, but it'll take everything I've got. I don't want to exhaust myself just yet." Ahead, the town entrance was shut, the heavy iron gates screeching open every few minutes to let someone in or out.

A woman carrying an armload of cloth walked down the road towards them. Julianne reached out and caught her arm.

"What's going on at the gate?" she asked.

"Oh, that's just Master August. He's looking for someone, closed the gates right after the soldiers left and won't let anyone in or out unless he talks to them." She shrugged. "He let me in. I guess I look all innocent! Little does he know!" She directed a salacious wink at Marcus, who tugged at his collar.

She smiled and wandered off, touching her head briefly as Julianne wiped their conversation from her mind.

"Shit," she said.

Marcus rubbed her back. "Look, there has to be another way out."

"You're right. Seher will know." Julianne grimaced at the thought of walking all the way back to the theatre tents—every minute spent in the city was a minute they would need to make up trying to beat the army to Tahn. She had to warn her people.

"Seher's got her own stuff to worry about. I got this one." Marcus grabbed Julianne's hand and started running, stumbling to a halt outside Muir's seediest inn. He pushed open the door, ignoring the 'closed' placard stuck to it.

A man sat at one of the few tables not draped with sheets. Fine powder coated the room and Julianne coughed.

"We're closed for—" the man inside began.

"I'll give you this if you tell us how to get out of the city without passing through the gates." Marcus tossed a small bag of coins onto the table.

"What makes you think I'd know that?" the innkeeper asked warily.

"Because you didn't get hit with violations before the New Dawn moved in. That means you know who to bribe… and I'll bet my eye teeth you spent money on more than a blind eye to a few roaches."

"Marcus, don't worry." Julianne plucked the purse off the table. "I've got what we need."

"Sorry, bud." Marcus tipped an imaginary hat before turning to leave. "You snooze, you lose."

The bewildered innkeeper just sighed. "This town is going to hell," he muttered before going back to his paperwork.

Julianne directed Marcus to a nearby backstreet. "Behind that house," she said. "Look for a big drain."

It was under a stack of heavy-looking boxes that Julianne pushed aside with no effort.

"Nice cover," Marcus commented. "I wouldn't have looked under there back in my days as a city guard."

"Good thing no one from Muir did, either." Julianne waited for Marcus to lift the heavy iron cover on the drain, then jumped down.

"Do I want to know what I'm stepping in down here?" Marcus asked.

"Just water. This part of the city is prone to flooding, so there's a few of these drains about, at least according to the innkeeper's memories. Most are soldered shut, but some enterprising young chap left this one open in exchange for a hefty bribe a few years ago."

"Good." His boot squelched in something. "I still think there's more than just water down here, though."

"Don't think about it," Julianne suggested.

She held onto the barest trace of her magic, just enough to know if they had caught anyone's attention. Exhaustion gnawed at her bones, but she kept going, one muddy foot after the other.

She stumbled, once, and sagged against Marcus for a brief moment when he caught her. Then, slipping into a light trance, she asked him to lead. "Just hold my hand and guide me," she told him.

Her eyes began to droop as she threw herself into a meditation. Her magic reached out, and the world around her reached in, the two connected in a glorious feeling of serenity.

Energy leaked back into her body, slowly reversing the strain of her earlier magic use. Her breath came in a steady rhythm, matching her steps. Absorbed by the gentle splashes that filled her ears and the musty, heady scent of old water, she didn't notice when Marcus stopped.

"Woah, steady on," he said when she collided with him. "Looks like we're—oh, for fuck's sake."

He pounded his hand on the rusted old padlock holding the grate closed. Green grass and sunshine lay within arms' reach, but he pulled back. "Back to the bloody start."

"Not so fast, cranky." Julianne took the padlock and yanked the mechanism. The bolt slid out, and she twisted it open.

"How'd you do that?" Marcus asked. He took the lock from her and examined it. "The latch was filed. Gee, thanks for telling me so I could avoid looking like an idiot."

"Sorry," Julianne shrugged. "I didn't want to ruin that reputation of yours."

"Gee, thanks." He shoved at the bars and pushed open the final barrier between them and freedom from the city of Muir. "You think the horses will still be at the inn when we come back?"

"If we ever do, they'll have been sold off a long time ago." Julianne blinked in the sunlight and carefully waded through the knee-deep stream that lapped at the tunnel. "We'll just have to make as much speed as we can, with as little rest as possible."

"What are we waiting for, then?" Marcus asked. With a bounce like he had just stepped out of bed, he loped up the small riverbank and into the woods beyond.

CHAPTER THIRTY-SIX

Danil was deep in conversation with Tessa when he saw, through the eyes of a man behind him, Annie's head pop into the schoolroom. His heart sped up—she never ventured this far without a good reason.

"Annie!" he called, hurrying over to her. "Is everything ok?"

"Boy, something's brewing." She hesitated, pursing her wrinkled lips in thought. Then, she spat out a huff. "Just read my damned mind. It'll be quicker."

Danil took a slow breath. Then, he dipped into Annie's head, something Julianne had expressly forbidden to ensure their host's privacy.

He felt the stillness in the air, the quiet lack of birdsong. He felt the nervous hum of the horses in his bones. He saw Annie walk into town, tasting the air, passing Lilly on the street. The girl was frowning, her attention on something distant. Their eyes met, and Annie acknowledged the girl's unspoken wisdom.

Something is coming.

It was more feeling than thought, a knowledge that something in this village, this place where she knew every breath and every sigh, was wrong.

Danil's muscles tightened and his stomach clenched. Annie didn't have much magic. She couldn't see the future or read the wind. She had something better than a connection to the etheric: good, old fashioned wisdom and intuition.

Years of living in a place that had etched itself into her bones made her hyper-aware of the slightest changes. That she was worried could only mean one thing.

"They're coming," he whispered.

Annie's shoulders slumped in relief. She had worried he wouldn't believe her, would write off her concerns as senile worry. *You were right,* she thought, picturing Julianne. *You have good people.*

"That she does," Danil grinned. "Though, they're about to become very *busy* people."

A smile quirked Annie's lips. "You just tell me what needs doing. If nothing else, I can still lift a shovel."

Chuckling at her eagerness, Danil waved her down. "No, leave the fighting to us. We need you to take the children, if you can?"

She nodded, straightening her shoulders as she disappeared out the front door, her blustering yell loud enough for them to hear inside. "Peterson! I see you there. Go holler up Marta and Janie's lasses, and tell them to help you round up the smaller ones. I'll go fetch young Conrad and his sister, and their neighbors. Meet me back here, and no mucking about, you hear?"

"Tessa," Danil turned back to the woman he had been talking to, his demeanor calm even as his breath quickened with worry. "Could you find Bastian for me? Tell him to meet me at Garrett's lookout. Oh, and tell him to bring Artemis."

"You don't want me to fetch the old man myself?" she asked, picking up her things.

Danil grabbed a sheet of parchment as it slid of the table. "If you think he'll come. Bastian's the only one who seems to be able to get him to do anything."

"Oh, I think I know what'll make old Artemis listen." She grinned, shoved her things in her bag, and pulled the drawstring. A shade of worry touched her eyes. "Danil, they're coming, aren't they?"

"I don't know, but either way, we'll be ready."

He watched her go, heart tearing as he wondered if he had told her the truth. Were they ready? *Well*, he thought, *we're about to find out.*

Confident that Tessa would do as he asked, Danil grabbed his cane and set off for the town gates, where Bette would be training. He didn't use the thin stick—at this time of day, the town was buzzing with people dashing between lessons with mystics and soldiers, tending to their houses and businesses and helping Francis build the wall.

"Bette!" he called when he spotted her. She turned from the man she was helping, passing him back the short spear and stomping over to Danil. He skimmed her mind, reading thoughts that mirrored her quickly changing expression.

What's this bastard want now, aye? Always fapping about—wait. No, he looks worried. Something's wrong. Ach, it's that bastard army I bet.

"What is it?" she snapped.

"That bastard army." She gave him a withering glare, but it didn't hide her sudden anxiety. "At least, I think so. Annie said... well, she had a 'feeling'."

"Aye, that's as clear as an arrow in the face for me. She knows what she's on about." Bette turned to look at the neat rows of soldiers, lined up and ready to spar. "Ye told Garrett yet?" she asked out of the side of her mouth.

Danil shook his head. "Just found out myself. I'll go there next."

"Weapons *DOWN!*" she yelled, the sudden, loud cry making Danil jump.

They poked up in surprise, but didn't hesitate to carefully

place their spears on the ground in front of them and stand to attention.

"All of ye, report to Garrett and tell him I sent ye for extra duty. If even one of ye doesn't make it ta that wall, I'll take ye over me knee and paddle yer ass."

"Aye, Captain!" They saluted, one hand to their head and one to their chest, then marched off at a quick trot.

"Take yer bloody weapons ye dipshits!" she screamed. The line disintegrated as they dashed back to grab their spears, then run off to the wall.

"Bastard fuck me up the ass. They do good under orders, but they're dumb as dog shit." Bette walked forward to grab her own weapons.

She stabbed a short sword into the scabbard on her belt, then dropped a knife down each boot. A thin rapier, the length of her short forearm, tucked down the back of her shirt. Then, grabbing two half-length spears, she thumped their butts on the ground and clicked her heels.

"What are your orders?" she asked briskly.

"Do… whatever you think is best? Hell, Bette, don't ask me for battle advice." He strode away in the same direction the soldiers had run. "But if I was going to offer it, it would run along the lines of 'don't get killed'!"

CHAPTER THIRTY-SEVEN

Garrett eyed the sudden influx of soldiers Bette had sent. It was a bad sign—the worst kind of sign. Whatever they had been preparing for the last few days was here.

"Lilly," he said to the girl next to him. "Remember what we talked about?"

She nodded. "You want me to do it now, don't you?" She shivered, scared of what was coming, but embraced her magic. Her eyes turned green.

Garrett beckoned to Sharne. "Fuck the guard, I want you lot on the wall! No point watching those bastards waltz on in. Go on, get to it!"

"Aye, Captain!" They deposited their weapons into one of the barrels at the guardhouse, then scurried off to find Francis.

Atop the small tower—the wall wasn't nearly as high as he liked, but damned if he was stupid enough to ask for a guard tower that would make him a sitting duck—he scanned the forest outside the little town. All was quiet.

"Anything yet?" he murmured.

He prayed this would work. When he had suggested to

Bastian that Lilly and her bird could act as scouts, Bastian hadn't exactly embraced the idea. In fact, the words 'stupid and danger-ous' may have passed his lips.

Thankfully, Garrett had the foresight to ask in front of Lilly herself, and once she had gotten the idea in her head, there was no dissuading her.

Lilly grunted. "Tarchus was eating. He didn't want me to interrupt him, and now he's being a jerk. He'll do it, though. He can tell something is in the air, and he wants to know, too."

A flock of birds erupted from the trees, squawking and flap-ping their way over the town. Garrett shuddered. Whatever had scared them was scaring him, too.

Cries behind him heralded Bette and Danil's arrival. He called out to catch their attention. "Up here!"

The three climbed the rickety tower and crowded onto the narrow platform. It didn't run the full length of the wall, but gave a good vantage point for some spear throwers and lookouts.

"What's going on?" Garrett asked.

"We're about to find out," Danil panted. He looked like he had been running. "Lilly? What are you doing here?"

"I'm a lookout, Danil! Tarchus is flying now... oh." Her smile dropped away and her face paled. "There's an army coming."

Lilly looked at the sky, green eyes sparkling as she read the images sent by the bird. "Tarchus thinks they're slow and ugly, but there are a lot of them. More than a pack, closer to a herd. They ride horses with broken spirits, and they sparkle like the stones his wife-bird uses in their nest."

Garrett shot Danil a look. "It's an army," Danil explained. "On horseback, with shiny armor, by the sound of it. I can see the images in her head, but the bird has distorted them, and I can't really understand the details."

"It's because he's distracted," Lilly said. "He wants to go look at the other humans."

"What other humans?" Bette asked warily.

"Running behind. They are a pack—not as many, and they work together well. Tarchus says… he says one is like me! And there are two more, walking slow. Oh, they're safe!" Lilly's eyes danced with excitement.

Danil broke into a grin. "I see them. It's Julianne and Marcus, but they're miles behind the army. Lilly, get Tarchus to fly back so I can get a sense of the distance."

Lilly nodded absently. The two stood, side by side, one with green eyes and one with white. Lilly's eyelids drooped as she slipped into the bird's head. Danil's did the same as he watched inside Lilly's. Though he couldn't communicate with the bird directly, he could see the images conveyed to Lilly and translate them for everyone else.

"They won't make it here until dark," Danil said. "With luck, they won't attack until morning. I wouldn't bank on it, though."

Garrett clicked his tongue. He really could have used a few extra days to prepare for this, but wasn't that always the case in battle?

"We'll be ready," Bette said with a giant grin.

"Lass, I know yer excited, but could ye please not look so happy ta start a fight that might get me head separated from me shoulders?" Garrett asked her.

"Bah, if that happened, I'd never forgive ye. Ye'd bloody deserve it for bein' in a stupid place at a stupid time, though, so no great loss." Bette planted one of her spears down, tip first, and leaned on it comfortably.

"No great—ach, ye nasty wench. No loss except the bloody hundreds of enemies I'd have taken down with me wee sword!" Garrett said with a scowl.

"Hundreds? If yer dumb enough ta die at the start, I'd wager ye wouldn't have taken out more than six on yer own anyway!"

"Yer a cheeky bitch. Wanna make a wager?"

"Hey, wait a bitch-damned minute, you two," Danil interjected. "No betting against each other—not unless you do it properly. I'll put my whole purse on Bette, hands down."

From below, a shout filtered up. "Hey, boys, the rearick are gonna face off against an army! They're taking wagers!"

That caused a commotion and soon, the chatter grew.

"My money's on the girl!"

"Yeah, I'll drop two gold coins on Bette."

"Alrighty then, lads! See Mack over there, drop your coins off. Five to one odds that Bette beats Garrett, sound fair!"

The chorus of agreement cause Garrett's blood to rise. Ok, so those odds might be fair, but at least half of those men betting against him were his!

"Pipe down ye bastards! If yer gonna make me feel like a useless twat, can ye do it where I can't hear ye?" he bellowed down.

Laughter exploded and the betting frenzy increased. Bette pressed her lips together, but couldn't hold back a chuckle. "Best ye show 'em up, rearick, or ye'll never live it down."

"Aye," Garrett said morosely. "Yer lucky I'm not a lesser man, or I'd ask ye ta throw a few kills my way."

"Yer the one that's lucky. If ye ask me that, I'll kill ye meself."

Garrett grinned. "Atta girl. Nothing like a good challenge, aye?"

Shaking his head and hoping his money was safe, Danil made his farewells. "I still have to brief Bastian, cajole Artemis into fighting, get Lilly to safety and figure out who the group behind the army is."

"Not to mention feed us," Garrett said.

Danil paused. "Feed you?"

"Aye. If my men are pulling a long shift and sleeping on the ground tonight, ye'd best sort some good rations for them so they're not fighting on empty bellies."

"Very well, I'll see what I can do."

Garrett watched Danil go, then turned to Bette. "Do ye think the men can live through this?" he asked.

"Not likely to get out without some casualties," she said. "But have some trust, old man. We've taught them well. They'll do what they need to."

"Aye." Garrett turned back out to look at the still, dark forest. "That they will."

CHAPTER THIRTY-EIGHT

The first sign something was coming was the animals. A herd of deer ran out of the forest, erupting from the woods at a sprint and circling towards the south when they saw the walled-off city of Tahn. Then, birds tore towards the sky, disrupted from their quiet homes by... something.

"They're getting closer," Bette whispered to Garrett, squinting into the distance. The grey landscape had been leached of color by the dropping sun, and long shadows now stretched between Tahn and the woods that shaded the way towards Muir.

"Aye."

They hadn't discussed who would stand guard that night. They didn't need to. Rearick were trained to fight on little food and less sleep, to push on through weariness and pain to complete whatever mission lay ahead, whether it was picking clean a deep mine or escorting a shipment between towns.

They both intended to see out this night, and the fight that would come, if not now, then in the morning.

"Ye think they'll attack when they get here?" Bette asked. She might be the better fighter, but she had never seen battle.

Garrett had. Swept up in the revolution that freed the city of

Arcadia, he had seen battle lines drawn, seen people die for a cause they believed in. It hadn't been pretty, but it had worked.

"Aye," he said simply. George would be a fool to let his men fight after a day and a half slog on foot or on horseback, but he'd be a bigger one to let them sit and wait to be attacked in the night.

He paced along the ledge behind the wall. The blasted, godforsaken, gift of a wall. He had no idea how Francis had gotten it up so fast, or how Lilly had convinced an entire wolf pack to dig a trench beyond it, but it was their first line of defense.

The men had eaten well that afternoon—early enough that they wouldn't puke on their boots when they saw the army awaiting them, late enough that it wouldn't matter if they missed breakfast.

The women of the town had fawned over the brave members of the new Tahn Guard, delivering home cooked meals and showering them with compliments. That had lifted the spirits of the terrified soldiers and left the town feeling uplifted and confident.

Most of the army was asleep, bunked in neighboring houses, or wrapped in blankets along the nearby roads, close enough to spring into action if an attack came.

A barking dog shattered the still, night air. Howls from a wolf pack outside joined him. More birds took flight, rising into the air and darting off to find a more secure sleeping place for the night.

"Garrett?" Bette said in a low voice. "Can you see the trees?"

Five minutes ago, the individual trunks had been so deep in shadows, even under the bright moon, that the forest looked like a giant swathe of unbroken blackness. Now, Garrett could make out each tree's silhouette. Something was casting a light from behind them. There was only one thing it could be.

"Aye. Don't raise the alarm. Go get the boys on the quiet, like."

She nodded and slipped way.

The only sign that she had done it was the occasional scrape of boots on stone, or the soft clink of metal as they carefully and quietly got ready.

"Lads, heads down," Garrett called in a quiet whisper along the barricade.

Obediently, the soldiers on guard—even Sharne, who at any other time might have thumped him for calling him a lad—ducked down low.

From outside, it would look like the flimsy wall was unmanned.

The heavy stomp of marching boots reached Garrett's ears just as Bette slid back in next to him. "I sent a runner to the mystics," she whispered. "And told him to warn Annie after that."

"Good, good." Garrett crept along the wall, listening to the rhythm of the approaching hoofbeats.

"They think we're sleeping on the job!" he said in a loud whisper. "Let's let them keep thinkin' it, aye?"

They stayed low, waiting until the horses pulled up to a whinnying stop before the gates. Garrett could tell the men outside were trying to be quiet. They spoke in whispers, hushed their nags and snapped at each other for the noise they made.

However, an army of soldiers is not an easy thing to keep silent. Without even sticking his head up, Garrett could tell where they were.

He looked around to make sure his own men were in position. Sure enough, they lined the battlements and clustered below. In fact, Garrett realized, there were more than just the soldiers milling around the protective wall.

"Bette, what the fuck are they doing down there?" he asked in a low voice.

She shrugged. "Exactly what I would have done."

The few nearby windows that let out the soft glow of lantern light let Garrett pick out a few of them. They were women, armed with shovels and pitchforks, their dresses tied above their knees, so they wouldn't trip and hair in neat braids, away from hands that might grab a chunk in a fight.

"Why the bloody hell wouldn't they train, then?" he asked.

She shrugged. "Too damn busy. Doesn't mean they won't be able to help."

"Fair enough." He knew better than to argue with her over it.

Outside, the army was becoming louder and more restless. He could hear the nasty little lordling grumbling in discomfort, and he knew exactly when they decided to attack.

The horses bolted forwards. Garrett help his hand up, motioning his men to stay down. A dull scrape on the wall was his cue.

"*NOW!*" he screamed, and as one, the soldiers on the wall rose. Each one multiplied, splitting into multiple soldiers and making it look like they had three times the number of people on guard.

"Bloody mystics," Garrett snorted, glad they had come to lend a hand.

The Tahn Guard lifted spears, stabbing the men who climbed the sole ladder they had brought with them. They threw them, piercing the throats and bellies of horses and occasionally getting a man as well.

Archers sent back a volley of their own and three Tahn fighters fell, tumbling back off the battlement to the stones below. "Shields up, men!" Garrett screamed. The rough boards and tin-sheeted shields that had been hurriedly gathered were lifted, offering some protection from flying arrows.

Flames sprung up in the grass outside the wall. Horses reared and went into a frenzy. They bucked their riders off and tore away, trampling anyone who got in their way as the mysterious fire went out, leaving no sign of damage.

"Get them!" George screamed, sounding less than pleased with the resistance they had met. "Wipe those fuckers off the face of the planet! They killed my father, *KILL THEM!*"

"Wait," Bette asked, suddenly beside Garrett. "We did what? What the fuck did Julianne and Marcus do in Muir?"

Soldiers rushed to the wall, boosting each other up to reach the top, only to have fingers bashed or stabbed by those above. Some fell from the top, others buckled under the weight of their comrades.

Still, they came, piling over each other and climbing atop those who had fallen to a spear in the face, slowly gaining ground until the first men fell over the wall and into the city.

"For Tahn!" a scream came below, followed by a sickening crunch right under Garrett's feet.

He whirled and chopped off the arm of a man attempting to scale the wall, then stabbed his sword through the eye of another.

"Do limbs count?" He had to scream to be heard, looking frantically around for the man who was taking the wagers earlier.

"Don't be stupid!" came the shouted answer.

Cursing, Garrett debated climbing over the wall to find the owner of the arm he now held, but satisfied himself with beating it over the head of another soldier before opening his throat.

He moved over towards Bette, tripping over three dead men in a pile.

"Six." She leaned over, hauled a man up by the scruff of his neck, and slammed the hilt of her sword down into his face. It exploded, gore coating her armor. "Seven," she grunted.

"Oh, fuck," Garrett muttered. He waited for another head to pop up and when none came, he peered over to see the crowd below him had moved on already.

Further along the wall, George's soldiers had managed to ram a part of the wall hard enough that it bowed inwards. "They're about to breach the wall!" he yelled to those nearby. Then, he added to himself, "If I run out of people to kill, I'm fucked!"

He eyed the low lip of the wall, the only thing between him and the army outside. "Only one way to fix it. *LOOK OUT BELOW!*" he screamed, then vaulted over the wall.

He landed on his feet, planting solidly into the ground. Three soldiers looked up, startled. One grinned. "Looks like they're making it easy and coming to us," he sniggered.

"Aye," Garrett grunted as he took down the first one. "Easy for me, that is." A duck and a swipe spilled the second man's guts, and a fast thrust left the sniggering soldier on his knees, watching the battle as he died.

"Four, five, six," he counted, trying to remember if he had seen the armless one at the bottom of the wall. He would have to go and check later. He couldn't leave a kill uncounted, after all.

"Ready yerselves, bastards, I'm coming for ye!" he hollered before dashing into the mass of enemy soldiers.

CHAPTER THIRTY-NINE

Marcus spurred his horse on, briefly looking back to check the others were keeping up.

Julianne was behind him, urging her horse on next to Madam Seher. The theatre leader had met them on the road and insisted on leading some of her people to the battle for Tahn.

Behind the women, Mathias, a green-eyed nature magician and a man with the black eyes of a physical user followed. Marcus knew the nature mage was keeping the horses going, while the other was dampening the sound of their hoofbeats.

They weren't bringing an army, but Marcus hoped they would be enough. They had passed the rest of the theatre troupe on the road, hurriedly speaking with Lord George who was still dazed at the events.

Unable to crack his mind, Rogan had eventually locked him up. Rogan had convinced anyone who asked that they had just seen Lord George a few minutes ago, or earlier that day. His absence wasn't noted, and the lord himself had failed in all attempts to escape.

Seher's people had rescued him, sneaking into the manor and releasing him from the dungeon right by Julianne and Marcus.

She still hadn't explained how that had happened. Surely, she would have noticed him when she had used her magic down there?

How far? Madam Seher sent to him.

He used the trick that let Julianne through his thoughts so she could read his answer. He thought about the trip they had made, and the road they would need to ride down to return to Tahn.

Good. Seher had read his mind, then, was satisfied they were close.

Grimly, Marcus ducked his head to avoid a low branch. Speed was of the essence. George Junior was too far ahead for them to warn Tahn he was coming, but they could still join the fight.

Tahn would be at battle by now, and Marcus wouldn't miss it for the world. A familiar old battle lust crept through Marcus's bones. It wasn't a want to kill—he hated that as much as Julianne and her mystics.

This was a craving for fast, precise movement, danger that heightened the senses. The noise and confusion that would melt away as he found his center, like all good fighters, and embrace the years of training he had gone through.

Hearing a low rumble ahead, Marcus yanked on his reins and his horse skidded to a stop, the others halting beside him. One hand up, he gestured for them to listen.

"Battle," Julianne said softly.

Despite her hate for a wasted life, Marcus could see the flush of excitement on her cheeks, even under the washed-out colors of the moonlit night.

"I'll race you," he said.

Before he could move, her horse bounded onto the road ahead of him, kicking a cloud of road dust up in his face.

"Oh, you're *on*, mystic!" he muttered. With a wild grin, he set off after her.

By the time he had caught up, she had already met with her

first opponent. A clean swipe with her staff felled the surprised soldier.

It's getting hairy up there, Julianne sent to Marcus. *Garrett is trapped near the wall, south of the main road in. See to him. Stupid rearick.*

Nodding, Marcus peeled off in a southerly direction. He could easily make out the cluster of soldiers who had separated from the rest of the army, bunched up beneath a glossy white wall.

Where the fuck did that come from? Marcus wondered as he headed towards it. Just as he pulled back to slow his horse, a loud, warbling cry erupted from the middle of the pack.

"Garrett!" he yelled, just as an armored fighter was thrown back from the others. Marcus aimed his magitech rifle and pressed the button on the side. It landed square in the back of a man trying to reach over his companions with a lance.

Marcus's target crumpled, his armor now sporting a deep, crumpled indentation surrounded by scorch marks.

The blinding flash was enough to catch the attention of the other soldiers. Some turned, and Marcus whacked the nearest across the jaw. He, too, fell to the ground.

Pivoting to avoid a sharp sword aimed for his throat, then darting away from a lance, Marcus yelled again. "Rearick?"

"Don't ye fucking *DARE* steal my kills, ye piss-born son of a donkey-faced prostitute."

How does he have the breath to swear like that? Marcus jabbed at another fighter, then shoved him back with a boot planted in the chest.

He debated tossing his weapon—it wasn't suited for close combat, it took too long to recharge. Still, he didn't relish being on the other end of it.

Using the blunt, useless weapon to punch a man in the balls, Marcus took a running jump. He leaped over the bent-over soldier, used him as a platform, and threw himself towards the wall.

He landed, fell forwards and tumbled to his feet.

"I fucking told ye, fuck off!" Garrett panted. He stabbed his sword, disemboweling one soldier while Marcus throat-punched his neighbor.

"Julianne sent me over. Said you're trapped. And stupid." Now back to back with Garrett, the two started inching their way out of the cluster of fighting and away from the pile of bodies Garrett had amassed.

"Aye, that's likely ta be—here, take that to the face, ye boil-faced pimple licker—true. Never was known fer me brains."

"You gonna tell me what you were doing?" Marcus asked.

Garrett stopped and looked at him, kicking a heavy boot at the knee of a man who got too close. "I'm counting me kills, ye dumb twat! Make sure ye take note of yer own, I don't want Bette thinkin' I cheated!"

"Right." Realizing what was going on—some kind of rivalry between the two—Marcus focused on the fighting. There were only four men left now.

Marcus's weapon whirred, and he shot it again, this time annihilating a man's face. A moment later, another soldier burst into flames.

"What was—ahh, FUCK! I was just about to kill that one! Who the fuck did that? I'll fucking kill him." Garrett looked around, wild-eyed, as the three remaining enemies looked at each other, then bolted for the safety of the army. He threw his arms in the air. "And now ye fucking scared the pussies away."

He took off running after them, Marcus hot on his heels. Soon they were joined by a third man—Francis.

"If that were you setting me targets on fire, yer dead when this is over," Garrett gasped. He stumbled to a stop, and Marcus and Francis looked at him in alarm. Hands on knees, he took three gasping breaths, then shot off again.

"Not me. I couldn't do that, not in a million years!" Francis protested.

"Must be Jakob," Marcus said. He eyed Francis, the only one of them that wasn't almost blue from lack of air.

"Who the fuck is Jakob?" Garrett asked. "Never mind. He'll be *dead Jakob* when I'm done."

They slammed into the main fighting force again, then scrambled back as three wolves leaped in beside them.

"The fuck?" Marcus asked.

The wolves ripped into George's soldiers, sending globs of flesh and blood into the air.

"Oh, Bastard," Garrett moaned. "The dogs are on our side, aren't they?"

"Seher brought a nature magician with her, so… I hope so?" Even Marcus was feeling a little green.

"We need to get to the wall," Francis said. He couldn't seem to pull his eyes away from the gory sight ahead. "They were climbing through the gap. That's why I came to get you, rearick."

"Yeah," Garrett murmured. "Let's be moving on, aye?"

CHAPTER FORTY

Julianne struck a solider with her staff. He grunted and doubled over in pain. A moment later he toppled, collapsing into a sleeping heap as Julianne's eyes cleared.

I'm coming for you, August. She sent the words to all the sweating, panting, heaving souls around her. August wouldn't hear it—he would be blocked, for sure. It would scare the shit out of anyone who could, though, and fear like that was infectious.

More than one man looked up, hackles raised as the whisper filtered through the battle rage.

I'm coming, and I will crush you and all who follow you.

She grabbed the mind of a man nearby and made him stop fighting. He stood, watching and feeling as a Tahn fighter slit his throat.

She stole the will of another, and he jumped out of her way. Then, another. Like a parting of the seas, Julianne walked through the battle untouched as men scrambled to make way for her.

She knew where he lurked on the other side of the battle, tucked in amongst his posse of mind-fucking mystics, all bonded in groups of three to reinforce their shields.

She couldn't sense them, but that little pocket of impenetrable nothing in the middle of the press of minds was conspicuous in itself.

When I find you, will I let the dogs tear your face off? Will I give you to the birds to strip clean?

She had heard the dogs and seen Mathias's glowing green eyes. Perhaps the soldiers had, too. One dropped his sword, looked around in a panic, and ran.

"Was that one you?" Madam Seher asked quietly.

Julianne shook her head minutely. The old woman was shielded tight and invisible under a spell that would force people not to notice her. She kept close to Julianne, out of the way of the soldiers.

I'm here, August. It's time. Time to face your sins.

The last few men scrambled out of her way without any nudging needed. They saw her eyes, heard her words. None were willing to stand against this beacon of justice that was coming for their corrupt leaders.

One man stood between her and August. A mystic, his eyes white and stance steady. The only man willing to face her.

Julianne lifted her staff and brought it down on his head and he folded to the ground.

A burst of magical energy, assisted by a whispered phrase, sent the surrounding soldiers running in terror. Black hands clutched at their hearts, ripped at their dreams as they stumbled away, weeping and screaming.

"August."

All that remained were four mystics, August, and a white-faced, sniveling Lord George. *The Third,* Julianne amended silently. What little she knew of his father made her wonder how his prodigy had turned out so poorly.

August fell back, trembling. "You can't touch me," he said. "You can't break my shields."

"A shield." Julianne launched forwards, slamming her staff on the shoulder of a woman in blue. "Is only." She whipped sideways, winding another. "As good." Jabbing forwards, she cracked the ribs of a man. "As its owner." In a final whirlwind, she struck the last man in the head.

Hearing a swish, Julianne glanced back to see Madam Seher removing a thin dagger from the throat of the soldier who'd tried to sneak up on her. She nodded her thanks.

August yelped, realizing his shield was no longer reinforced. "George? George, I demand you help me. Kill her!"

"A shield is only as good as its owner," George said, baring yellow teeth in an evil grin. Julianne dropped the compulsion, and he sank to his knees, shaking. "Oh, fuck, she's in my head!" he whimpered. "Fuck. Fuck. Fuck."

Clearly, George had been relying on his innate ability to shield for some time, and hadn't realized how fragile it really was.

"August, you stand charged with tyranny, despotism, and the complete disregard of Temple stricture. How plead you?"

"I didn't… he made me do it!" August trembled, and he sucked in a sharp breath, phlegm catching in his throat.

"Rogan never visited Tahn. Don't blame him for your actions there. How do you plead?"

"I didn't—" August's clothes erupted into flames. He screamed, clutching at the fabric and dropping to the ground, kicking in agony as his hair caught fire. The stench of burning flesh filled Julianne's nostrils, and she cut the sensation off.

"Who was that?" Seher snapped.

Francis stepped out of the watching crowd, one hand raised as he twisted his fingers in a tight circle. Heat billowed as the flames flared blue. August's cries dissipated as his body cooked.

No one spoke until he was nothing but a charred pile of bone and ash, toothy skull staring up with an eerie grin.

Francis walked over and stomped on the blackened head. It

crumbled into dust. "He killed my Danielle." He turned to Julianne. "It wasn't my place, but I won't apologize."

"I am not your ruler," Julianne said. "I am not judge, nor jury. It was not my place to decide his fate. You are the voice of this town, and the people he hurt. It was your place, and your right."

Francis looked to the sky, where smoke still trailed from the extinguished fire. A tear slid down his cheek. "I did it, Danielle. He won't hurt anyone again."

Then, he walked away into the city, disappearing behind the bright, white wall.

CHAPTER FORTY-ONE

Garrett knocked back his drink in one long pull, then wiped the foam from his whiskers. "So, it's a tie, then?" he asked.

Bette slumped. "Fine. It's a tie. I suppose yer a reasonable fighter after all."

Danil sank his head into his hands. "What the hell are we going to do?"

"About the New Dawn?" Julianne asked. "I don't know."

"No, about those two!" Danil shook a hand at the rearick. Garrett looked offended, Bette just grinned. "Next thing you know they'll be marching to bloody Muir to see who can kill Rogan first!"

Bette sat up. "Aye, now that's an idea!"

Julianne laughed. "Glad you'll be at my side. It won't be an easy fight."

Marcus rubbed his face. "Really? We ran all that way to get from Muir to Tahn, and now you're gonna make me go back?"

She nodded. "This time we'll make a better plan, though. And we'll have help."

"Aye, lassie, that ye will!" Garrett slammed his mug down and gestured for Mary to bring a refill. When Bette kicked him, he groaned and stood. "Fine, I'll get it. Who else needs another?"

As he strolled away to the bar to ask for three more ales, Julianne rubbed her eyes and yawned.

"Ye did a good thing, Julianne," Bette whispered. "But I don't think ye know how good. This town was more than saved. Ye liberated it. Not from the Dawn itself, but from the memory of them, from the feeling of being helpless."

Julianne's eyes burned and her throat ached. She had worried so much about dragging the fragile village into a battle so soon after what they had faced. It was good to know she had done the right thing.

They hadn't won the war yet, but they would. She was sure of it.

FINIS

waves excitedly Hi guys! Wow, I'm so super incredibly excited today! Dawn of Destiny (the book before this one) is due to release TOMORROW! For you guys, that's at least a week ago. Or more, because I live in the land of tomorrow, thanks to crazy time zones.

If you're confused, join the club!

So, I'm sitting (pacing) calmly (frantically) while sipping water (hot water, with coffee, milk and sugar added) and waiting for the world to see my new story. By the time you get to these notes, you'll know if you love Julianne or hate her. I'm guessing you at least like her a bit, if you got this far.

My little team is so much fun to play with. Bette just kicks ass and doesn't stop to apologise, and in a lot of ways, is like the prim and proper Annie. Danil and Marcus are a bit alike, but Bastian I think will turn out to be a lot smarter than most of them expected. Though the school he wants to set up is just a wish for now, I'd like to make it happen one day in the future.

Book three is still coming along quickly, after a few days interruption because of some very sick kids. I'm getting it done as fast as I can, so I can... you know, write another one!

I'm really looking forwards to next year in the KGU - when we move, my smallest kid will start kindy, and I'll have a couple of days every week JUST for writing! Which is great, because I've got sooo many more book ideas for Tahn and the mystics!

I guess I'd better run, but before I go, a quick update on the epic battle I'm fighting with Michael... I think I lost. It was close, but his poor taste has spread like a wonky nanocyte and infected too many for us to stand against him. Pineapple pizza lost.

-Amy

Thank you, I cannot express my appreciation enough that not only did you pick up the second book, but you read it all the way to the end and NOW, you're reading this as well. Since this book is part of a series, I am presuming you have blessed us by reading them both and what a fantastic feeling that is for any author!

I'm going to speak a bit about Amy and her ride this last week or so and to do that, I have to give you some behind-the-scenes information to set this up.

First, when we set up a book for sale, we have three pages of information to fill out. That information includes the title, series name, authors / editors / forward (if you want to add any of this) the blurb, keyword search terms, two categories, the book file, the cover file (separate), publisher information and finally price information.

You set another couple of preferences (inside Kindle Unlimited or not) and earning percentage (35% or 70%). It might seem a bit odd, "Why not always choose 70%?"

Well, if you have a book priced between $0.99 (the lowest) and $2.98 or more than $9.99 you MUST choose 35%. One of the benefits of 35% is Amazon does not charge us a fee for each download of the book. Typically, for a 70,000 word book with a file size for the cover of about 800k or so, we will be charged $0.05 per download.

However, if we have something with a LOT of pictures, we could choose to pay 35% and not be charged for the download fees which have the possibility of causing us to lose money on those books.

Once we have all of this information plugged in, we hit a "Submit" button and Amazon SWOOSHES it away to be placed "In Review."

If we have offered the appropriate sacrifices, don't have anything that looks wrong to the Amazon algorithms, the queue to be reviewed is short then we could have our books out in an hour or two and working to be sold around the world.

That's damned impressive!

But, occasionally something doesn't go to plan and a book is perhaps flagged for more review or we just have bad luck and it takes FOREVER. (Which, to us is anything over 45 minutes.)

Now, I get back to Amy.

Amy lives in Australia, so she is already one day ahead of us most of the time and when she is anxiously awaiting a Friday release, that's pretty much Saturday to her.

So, we setup and release her first book last week and she is already exhausted, but excited to see it go up on the store.

The only problem is it didn't release quickly. So, Amy is already tired, a day ahead and Amazon isn't pushing our book out.

Hour after hour she waits, biting her nails. Finally, she has to succumb to exhaustion and sleep. It took FOREVER for the book to come out, and when it did, it's already Saturday here in the states.

Not a great day to release a new book, by the way.

However, she has an excellent attitude and a really wonderful spirit and I have to say I'm blessed to be collaborating with her, CM Raymond and LE Barbant on the New Dawn series.

Thank you Amy, for your patience, your humor and your sarcastic and funny-as-hell Australian wit!

Ad Aeternitatem,
Michael

CONNECT WITH THE AUTHORS

Amy Hopkins Social
Website:
https://amyhopkinsauthor.com
Facebook:
https://www.facebook.com/thespellscribe

Connect with Michael Anderle

Website: http://lmbpn.com
Email List: http://lmbpn.com/email/

Social Media:

https://www.facebook.com/LMBPNPublishing
https://twitter.com/lmbpn
https://www.instagram.com/lmbpn_publishing/
https://www.bookbub.com/authors/michael-anderle